THE BLUE CIRCUS

THE BLUE CIRCUS

Translated by Sheila Fischman

Jacques Savoie

Originally published as *Le cirque bleu*
by Les éditions de la courte échelle inc.
copyright © Jacques Savoie, 1995
English translation copyright
© Sheila Fischman, 1997

All rights reserved. The use of any part of this publication, reproduced, transmitted in any form or by any means, electronic, mechanical, photocopying, recording, or otherwise, or stored in a retrieval system, without the prior written consent of the publisher — or, in case of photocopying or other reprographic copying, a licence from Canadian Reprography Collective — is an infringement of the copyright law.

This translation was completed and published with the support of the Canada Council. The publisher also gratefully acknowledges the support of the Ontario Arts Council and the Department of Canadian Heritage.

Cover design by Pekoe Jones,
from an illustration by Geneviève Côté.

Author photo by Robert Laliberté.

Printed and bound in Canada.

CORMORANT BOOKS INC.
RR 1
DUNVEGAN, ONTARIO
CANADA K0C 1J0

Canadian Cataloguing in Publication Data

Savoie, Jacques, 1951-
[Le cirque bleu. English]
The blue circus

Translation of: Le cirque bleu.
ISBN 1-896951-04-X

I. Fischman, Sheila II. Title. III. Title: Le cirque bleu. English.

PS8587.A388C5713 1997   C843'.54   C97-900895-6
PQ3919.2.S358C5713 1997

for Francis M.
for Pascale and Édith

Chapter 1
The Ringmaster

I just got in on the six o'clock train, the one from Chicago. Montreal is still asleep and I wonder what I'm doing in this city. Three days ago I did my act with Barnum and Bailey for the last time: a simple once around the ring with an elephant. While the technicians were dismantling the lions' cage and getting ready for the next act, I took a little spin with a big animal named Lucky — while playing the flute. Actually, the instrument I use is nothing like a flute, it's a kind of farandole; it has sections of pipe welded together, with violin strings and a resonance board. You just speak into it and it makes music.

I claim that I don't know what I'm doing here, but deep down I do. I have a sister living around here somewhere. A half-sister, actually. I lost track of her quite a while ago. I don't know where she is or what she does. She'd be twenty-nine or thirty now. Probably settled down in the suburbs. With children.

The circus wasn't always like that. I mean, I didn't always just do routine acts. Only three months ago I was teamed up with a knife-thrower. A gypsy known to everyone as Bobby. He had a terrifically successful act — throwing daggers at his niece, a very beautiful girl called Sally, whom he'd brought over from somewhere in eastern Europe. I played the clown around the two of them while the knives flew. The act worked really well until one night in Oakland, California, when everything stopped! A muffled cry came down to us from the stands and suddenly the crowd was on its feet. It hurts just to think about it.

The station is nearly empty at this hour and I feel as if I'm under the big top. Men go back and forth, setting things up for the next performance. I often think about the circus. I imagine the ideal show: the music, the animals, the mimes and acrobats. I put on some wonderful acts. But as of today I'll have to settle for dreaming about it. I left Chicago so I could forget. Ever since I stepped onto this train, though, I feel as if I'm being observed, being followed. There was a glum-looking guy on the station platform. It wasn't Bobby, but there was a resemblance. And farther away there was a woman watching me. I'm sure I didn't imagine that. She was spying on me, I'm positive.

To shake them off I disappeared into the station. Instead of going to the checkroom for my suitcase, I made a stop in the bathroom, where I looked at people's reflections in the mirror. They were all minding their own business. Nothing to worry about. So I came out, found a quiet spot under a big window and since then I've been looking through the newspaper and sipping from this cup the waitress keeps filling. The customers having breakfast here look sad. Probably I do too. Which suits me fine, I don't want to stand out in the crowd.

The longer I look at the waitress, the more I find she

resembles Sally. Blonde hair and eyes of an unsettling blue. The costume's different, though. And the makeup. In her costume of light, Sally glowed like a beacon under the big top, while this woman gives off absolutely nothing.

I have to get in touch with my half-sister, Marthe, and her countless children. How can I find out if she kept her own name or if she uses her husband's? I could go to Éliane Street, at one time home to Victor Daguerre, a bookseller and the father we shared.

My eyes are glued to the newspaper though it's totally boring. I don't want to spend all day in this railway station, but I don't really know where to start.

Eight a.m. Too early to phone. Especially when you've been out of touch for ten years. At the checkroom, the sleepy employees can't find my suitcase. They gave me the case for my flute just now, the one I use in my act with the elephant. As for the rest, we'll see.

"Your suitcase will probably be on the next train. Come back later today."

That suitcase contains everything I need for the tricks I do. Costume, makeup, good-luck charms, balls for juggling. I'm lucky they gave me my instrument. But where shall I go? To the house on Éliane Street? Near the square, along Delorme Boulevard. There used to be some motels there. Maybe there still are. That would work out, since I used to know that neighbourhood like the back of my hand.

So I climb into a taxi, we travel along a wide boulevard, and I'm fascinated by all the changes. I've got my flute case on my knees and my eyes are glued to the window and I don't recognize a thing. It doesn't matter, though, the driver knows where we're going.

"Motel Émard? Sure it's still there! The park too ... if

you can call it a park!"

*

The Motel Émard is a long corridor, a gypsy caravan that stopped there a long time ago. They gave me a room at the very end, away from the traffic. I can't imagine living in a place like this. Yet I'm perfectly comfortable here. I've gone back to the station twice since yesterday. Still no word about my suitcase. As for the mystery surrounding my half-sister, it has gradually cleared up. In the phone book there's an M. Daguerre at 1444 Éliane Street. My theory about the suburbs and all the children is crumbling little by little. Like her father, Victor Daguerre, she must have opted for books.

I went to look at the house. It's in bad shape, but it's not alone. The whole neighbourhood looks run down. The more I think about it, the more I wonder why I want to see Marthe again. Really. What would we talk about? Even in the past we didn't get along all that well.

At the station I felt as if I were being followed. Now, though, I can sometimes forget about it. How could anyone know I'm here, in this dark motel room at the end of a long corridor? In fact, all I need to be perfectly happy is my suitcase ... and that small matter I want to ask Marthe about. But my half-sister is giving me stage-fright, as if I were about to make my entrance into the ring for the first time. Maybe it would be better if I phoned her. But then again, in the circus you don't make a phone call before you do your act.

Chapter 2
The Knife-Thrower

When he finally made up his mind to call, it was Marthe herself who answered. She was very happy to talk to him, to hear from him, but she was in a hurry. Her job at the library took up all her time and she suggested they get together later in the week, preferably in the morning. Saturday and Sunday were impossible. They finally agreed on Tuesday. The conversation was quite amicable but when he hung up he was still wondering why he had called.

The following Tuesday he was at the house well before the hour. He didn't understand what was driving him as he paced the little square, gazing at each of the buildings in turn, peering into store windows and admiring the few surviving trees. The bookseller's big house was a mere shadow of its former self. The white paint was yellowish now, the big veranda seemed about to cave in and, had it not been for the support the cornices seemed to provide, it would have looked like a galley sinking into the sea.

He had never lived in this house. It had belonged to

Geneviève Granger, Marthe's mother and Victor Daguerre's second wife, who had inherited it from her own father, an architect with a penchant for designing churches. Though Hugo had never lived here, he had a weakness for this house. Until his departure for the United States, he had secretly dreamed of living in it. Absorbed in his thoughts, he opened the gate and stepped inside the little garden. He was measuring the extent of the damage when the door opened before him.

"So soon?"

Marthe too was unrecognizable. A little plump, tousled hair — she could have been forty or forty-five. What shocked him more, though, was her housecoat. It was the same as Sally's: a kind of towel she'd wrap herself in before going on stage.

"I ... I wanted to see the old neighbourhood."

"Come in," she said. "I leave for work at ten but we've got time for a coffee. How long has it been?"

"Uhmm...."

"Let's see. My mother died four years ago and you must have been gone for five years by then."

"Ah! So your mother's dead?"

Hugo looked around him as he wiped his feet. She slipped into the kitchen.

"I'll be right back!"

The room matched his memories. Books everywhere. All over the chairs, the floor, the coffee table. Hundreds, thousands of books. But, strangely, they had not been arranged as Victor Daguerre would have had them. Rather, they formed uneven piles that suggested a miniature city.

She returned with a tray laden with coffee.

"Are you still with the circus?" she asked.

In the past her chubbiness had given her a

mischievous look, but now her middle-aged appearance made her seem rather serious. He went into the living-room and cleared one corner of the table, stroking the varnish along the grain of the wood. He had been in this room only once before and his memory of it was vague.

"I really must sort them out," she announced, as if she'd been reading his mind. "I ought to do some tidying but I can never find the time. There's so much to do at the library."

The daughter of the bookseller Victor Daguerre had become a librarian. It wasn't surprising. It was almost to be expected. Only the bathrobe was at odds with the image. She poured the first cup and he thought he saw her tremble.

"Now tell me, Hugo. What is it that brings you here?"

He squirmed on the sofa while she cleared a corner of the easy chair. The small table couldn't take any more of being used as a bookshelf and he hesitated before replying:

"The chalet. Papa's chalet up at the lake. I'd like to spend some time there. I wondered if ... I mean, if you'd mind if...."

"The chalet? You're not serious. I can't imagine there's anything left of it. All the land around it has been sold. All sorts of cabins have been put up. I haven't been there myself for five or six years."

"What about the lake?"

"Oh, the lake's still there. But it's not what it once was."

Hugo's jaw was clenched as he ran his hand over his face, finally saying:

"Actually I'm not even sure the lake would be enough to help me forget...."

"Forget what?"

They looked hard at one another for a moment. She sipped her coffee, wavering between curiosity and her desire to keep her distance. There was something dramatic about her face. Even when it was at rest you could sense an underlying impulsiveness.

"We haven't seen one another for years. So if you want us to understand each other you'll have to stop talking in riddles."

Her tone had hardened all at once. Marthe was carrying on like an offended librarian, while Hugo was trying to find the right words.

"It's just that ... you're wearing the same bathrobe as ...."

"Aha! So there's a woman involved. A love affair that turned sour, maybe? And you think you'll get over it by going to the lake?"

He shrugged and she took a sip of her coffee. Basically she was trying to cheer him up, shake him out of his melancholy. He looked so sad, this half-brother of hers, so full of remorse.

"Look, if it will make you happy you can have the keys. Go up to the chalet and make yourself at home. But I warn you, you'll be disappointed. The years have taken their toll. It's a hovel now. You won't even want to spend a night there."

"It's more than an unhappy love affair! I need to disappear, make people forget about me for a while."

She pulled her bathrobe across her chest and set her cup down on a corner of the table. You could read the emotion on her face.

"Wait, I want to be sure I understand. You met this woman in the circus. She dropped you and now you want to be alone. You need something to take your mind off what happened."

That was what she'd have liked to believe but it was not the case. He had thought she'd simply give him the keys and let him go. But he had forgotten that in the Daguerre family everything happened through words, through long explanations wherein every silence invariably led to another question.

"What is it you're trying to tell me?"

This time her tone was almost reproachful. Under other circumstances, he would have put an end to the conversation and left. But he didn't. For once he wanted to go all the way. So many things had happened since he'd left for the States.

"Her name was Sally. She came to America ten years ago with her uncle. Actually her name was Safiyya or something like that. She came from a gypsy family — twelve of them — who travelled all over Europe. She and her uncle spoke French together, with a very strange accent. They'd spent time in the south of France, at Saintes-Maries-de-la-Mer, I think. It was vague. At least she never talked about it. She called herself Sally because it sounded American and also because it helped her forget what had happened in the past. As for the uncle, I never knew his real name. He'd been a knife-thrower at fairs in Europe. He was thirty when he landed in the States and she was around eighteen. The two of them were always together. They were very close."

Hugo had said these last words in a hushed voice, as if afraid of hearing them himself. But there was no need to paint Marthe a picture. Bobby the knife-thrower slept with his niece. Charming.

"They joined Barnum through the stables ... I mean, that was the first job they had. Feeding the horses. Whenever he could, Bobby would slip behind the stands to watch the show. There was just one thing he wanted: to climb into the ring and get back to work.

"One day he took Sally to the dressing-rooms and showed her all the wonderful costumes: 'If you want to,' he told her, 'you can be part of my act.'

"She did want to and he took her into the ring. He showed her the nets, the wires, the floodlights. All she had to do was say yes and she'd have all America at her feet, applauding her every night.

"'But what do I have to do?' she asked.

"'Not a thing! Just stand against the wall and stay there without moving. While I throw knives.'"

Marthe was becoming fascinated by this story. The more he talked, the more his face brightened. This half-brother she remembered only vaguely was much more interesting than he'd seemed at first. She had thought he was shy, but he was nothing of the kind.

"Everyone has his own reasons for joining the circus. Everyone knows why he goes into the ring and risks his neck. In Sally's case, she was running away from something, I don't know what.... But apparently those knives that outlined her body day after day were a lesser evil compared to what she'd once known. She actually enjoyed them."

Marthe tried to break in, but he seemed not to notice and continued to talk without even stopping for breath. His delivery was rapid, as if he didn't want to stop.

"Their act went very well. Sally was beautiful and most of all she was determined. A perfect target, with that fragility that stirs pity in decent folks. When he was facing her, Bobby seemed menacing. He'd throw his ten knives and then Sally would emerge from her coffin of blades, run across the ring and kiss him. The kiss was very important. All at once the knife-thrower and his victim were one, they were human again. And the people in the stands would leap to their feet and applaud.

"This had been going on for a while when Sally and I met. That was in Louisville, Kentucky. She came to me because she was fascinated by clowns. She wanted to know how anybody could keep his makeup on all day and never show his real face. I babbled something, the first words that came into my head, and in her heavy accent she said: 'You're crazy, Hugo.' There was something affectionate in her voice, in the way she said it."

Now Marthe was only listening with one ear, holding back the question that had been burning her lips for some time. When he paused, she stepped in.

"What about you, Hugo, why did you join the circus?"

He wet his lips, considered a complicated answer, then stopped. He had started to say something and he didn't want to be diverted.

"In the beginning we were a ménage à trois. Sally couldn't distance herself from her uncle. But she still spent time with me. Nobody was in any position to judge the others and each of us adapted as best we could. The knife-thrower would have preferred to keep her to himself. But she was his niece and he was well aware that one day or another...."

By the end, Marthe was very touched by what Hugo told her. The uncommunicative boy, the withdrawn adolescent, had become someone else. An intriguing man, mysterious even, like those she sometimes encountered in books.

"One day, Bobby got this weird idea. A clown in a knife-throwing act would be fantastic. While he was doing his thing, I'd walk around between him and his niece, juggling three or four balls. Once, the knife would go past my back; the next time, right under my nose. I would bend down to pick up a ball I'd dropped and a third knife would whistle over my head. Bobby thought this was brilliant. I wasn't sure I agreed, but he and Sally talked me into giving it a try. The dance of death was as finely tuned as a violin. Before going on, Bobby would proclaim in his heavy accent: 'Anyvay, nothing is vorse than everything!' I thought this motto was rather sinister, but it had the virtue of getting rid of fear. From that point, everything seemed to happen at once. The music, the cries of the crowd, the knives flying in every direction, the balls I juggled above my head. In ten minutes it was over. Sally emerged from her tomb and kissed her uncle. Meanwhile I picked up my balls as if nothing had happened, and the audience shrieked with delight."

Hugo took a mouthful of coffee, left a slightly longer pause and was surprised when Marthe didn't ask any questions, didn't want any points cleared up.

"And then came Oakland. The circus had settled there for the winter and it was supposed to be closed for two weeks. I'd looked in the papers and found a little cottage on the coast. I wanted to spend some time there alone with Sally, but her uncle hit the roof. As long as we were at the circus, as long as she kept shuttling back and forth between his trailer and mine, everything was fine. But if we ran away together.... He started drinking and giving her a hard time. She said it wasn't serious, he'd calm down eventually. But he wouldn't budge, and I was scared. We always spoke French together and nobody else understood what we were saying. I was reluctant to go into the ring, but Sally finally persuaded me. She went back to see him, they had a talk, this time things were a little calmer and finally he barked: 'It's true. Nothing is vorse than everything.' It was as if nothing had happened."

Marthe was hanging onto his every word, but she was a little more nervous. She was obviously afraid of what was coming next. But still she asked:

"And then?"

"When we came into the ring, under the lights, with the music and everything ... it all seemed normal. Every time Bobby threw a knife, the crowd screamed. But after a moment I had the impression that something was happening. The knives were flying faster than usual. And every time, their direction startled me. Bobby and I had a code. I must never look at him when he was working. It was all supposed to be done blind. But this time it was too much. I looked up and I realized he was aiming at me. His eyes were black and there was something unsettling about his mouth. There was nothing Sally could do, she was blindfolded. So I threw myself to the ground and rolled outside the circles of light. A knife grazed my ear and as I was getting to my feet I heard a cry. A little muffled cry. Sally had collapsed at the base of the target and she was bleeding. The first-aid people came right away, an army of clowns was busy at the other end of the ring, and they carried out the body with the blindfold still in place."

Marthe grimaced. She was like a child before him. Her upper lip was quivering and she was moving her hand back and forth as if trying to erase what had just been said.

"Poor Hugo."

She would have taken him in her arms and consoled him, but he was keeping his distance. His account had been very moving. She'd have liked to touch him, reassure him. She did lay her hand on his knee. He shrank back.

"Sorry," she whispered, stiffening. "I only wanted to say.... I mean, if there's anything I can do for you ... the chalet, anything."

He nodded, looking rather pale now, and he seemed to be sorry about something. Having stripped himself bare, maybe. Having told her all this at their first meeting.

"If you want," Marthe insisted, "I could make room for you here for a few days. Saturdays and Sundays it's a little complicated but...."

"No, no. That's all right. I have a room. You know, Bobby's the kind who'll seek revenge. He was questioned in Oakland. They wanted to indict him there, but somehow or other he finally got off the hook. The circus was in Chicago when they let him go. That was why I left. I crossed the border at Windsor. I know he'll come looking for me. And I don't want to drag anyone else into it."

Marthe seemed less concerned about Bobby's threats than about Sally's death. There was a long silence, the kind in which you suddenly ask yourself what you're doing there. She leaned back in her chair and gazed at the ceiling.

"I'm serious, Hugo. We could fix a room for you upstairs."

Now it was he who was trembling. He was trembling because he was still surprised at what he had just said.

"You know, this is the first time I've told anyone the story. I mean ... it only happened a few weeks ago. And I haven't had a chance to talk about it."

She put a finger to her lips, as if she didn't want to hear the rest. In less than an hour she'd been transformed before his eyes. This woman who was a little too old for her years, this rather severe librarian who had opened her door to him, was now behaving affectionately. She ran her hand over his shoulder. The little hint of emotion was still there in her eyes, but now she was beaming. In fact she was altogether buoyant. He sank deeper into the sofa too and threw his head back. They gazed at the ceiling for a while, in silence.

*

It was a quarter to eleven when she announced that she had to leave. Again and again, Marthe suggested that he stay, that he move in at least for the day while he was waiting for some word about his suitcase. But Hugo had other plans.

She went to the bathroom, no longer insisting, and he approached the piles of books, which were intriguing him more and more. Behind the apparent disorder there was a logic to the way they were grouped. An intuitive arrangement of the kind children put in their drawings. In fact it could have been a child's drawing. Hugo picked up a few books, the ones on top. He opened them without trying to see the titles, mostly he simply touched them, and he couldn't help thinking about Victor Daguerre. It was as if he were upstairs, in a bedroom, getting ready to come down:

"What kind of mess have you got yourself into this time? Why can't you be like your sister? I can't figure you out. Can't you take an interest in something instead of always drifting?"

Hugo stepped back, brushing aside his father's ghost.

He picked up another book, a little farther away. It was printed on fine India paper and it was very silky to the touch. Again he merely turned the pages, thinking there was something sensual about doing so. He was alone here, surrounded by all these words — he who hadn't read three books in his entire life. There must be millions of pages here. Tons of sentences that would provide the answers to every question imaginable, to anything that could make anyone suffer. He felt out of place in this house, yet he was glad he'd come.

Marthe had donned her librarian's clothes and pulled her hair into a bun. When she came into the living-room from the bathroom, she was as considerate as before ... but her uniform created a distance between them.

"If you'd like, I could go up to the chalet with you next week. I have some time off. We could get together again."

She sipped some cold coffee, grimaced and added as if she'd been thinking it over for a long time:

"And as for that man, the knife-thrower, forget about him. He'll never find you here."

She was smiling broadly as she took her purse from its peg. And when her gaze fell on the book he was holding, she became all professional:

"Ah! Baudelaire...."

He didn't understand immediately and she had to point to the title.

"Baudelaire. You want to take Baudelaire with you?"

That hadn't really been his intention. He had held onto it because he liked its silky feel. But he didn't have the courage to admit that so he pretended to be pleased. They walked slowly through the little garden. Before she took her leave, though, Marthe returned to the attack:

"About the chalet — I hope you'll think it over.

Actually, I'd be curious myself to see what's left of it."

At the gate, they exchanged a kiss on the cheek, then went their separate ways.

Chapter 3
The Ringmaster (encore)

Nearly four days I've been here. And still waiting for my suitcase. I spend my days in this motel room and I only go out in the evening. The book by Baudelaire is on the bedside table, along with the Bible and the phone book. I haven't read a line yet, but now and then I stroke the silky pages.

The Motel Émard runs along the entire width of Number Nine. That's a green space that was laid out in the early sixties when an old dump was covered over with thousands of tons of earth. As there were already eight parks in the city, they didn't rack their brains to come up with a name for this one. Over the years it became known as Number Nine. People are quite fond of this big, treeless field whose shape is always changing.

At night I prowl around in the park. It has absolutely no charm. Trees don't grow there, the swings are rusty and the playground is as vast as it's always been. The perfect spot for a big top. But the park has another virtue too. It's exactly halfway between Victor Daguerre's house and mine. I mean the one where my mother and I lived, farther south, close to the river. The neighbourhood has been destroyed now — the better to rebuild it. My mother is dead and I've promised myself to go and see it — one of these days.

I used to come here sometimes with my father and my half-sister. Victor Daguerre wanted me to get to know Marthe, so he used to organize these little meetings. Our weird family had only a vacant lot as a playground and our favourite game was stealing the bookseller's attention for ourselves, fighting over it the way you fight over a toy. He was both the referee and the object of these matches.

There has always been rivalry between Marthe and me. Things weren't much better with my father. That was actually why I left, before there was a split. When she asked me why I'd chosen the circus, I was so afraid of replying that I just said the first thing that came into my head. I could have blamed it on books, on Victor Daguerre. I was such a delinquent, so totally useless to him, that I ran away. Yes, that was it. It was better for me to go somewhere else, for them to forget all about me. I was the child he'd had accidentally, the child who lived across the park in that depressing part of town, alone with his mother. He was too polite to tell me that. He'd have preferred that I not exist. He loved Marthe so much. Which was why I went away — but you don't come out and say a thing like that.

*

My suitcase is definitely lost. The checkroom attendants

at the station don't know what to say any more. At first they claimed that the suitcase didn't exist, since it didn't appear on any list of lost articles. Then they changed their minds and offered me reimbursement. I had to put down a figure, give a value to the medley of odds and ends. I claimed they were priceless treasures. They came up with all kinds of excuses because that was part of their job. Which didn't prevent them from settling with me for a thousand dollars.

So I've been here for a week now. In this same room, with the window looking out on the park. I could leave, go somewhere else, but I'm not sure that would be best. It would be nearly impossible to find me here; I'm so far from anything, at the end of my forgotten corridor, that I have trouble finding myself. When I think about Bobby, I'm convinced that he's suffering as much as I am. He must be shattered, torn apart, without Sally. I imagine him as paralysed with grief. The more I think about it, the more I feel that he's trying to forget me too. That he's probably trying to get over his own grief, in a motel room much like this one.

The picture I painted of him for Marthe may have been too harsh. He's not really an evil man, just different from the people you meet on the street. And he loved Sally. I didn't say this to my half-sister, but it was as if he revered her. And it was touching. As if they were each other's last hope, the last thing they could cling to.

Yesterday I bought myself some clothes and a new suitcase, and little by little I'm rebuilding my wardrobe. At first I wanted to store my things in the flute case, but when I got the instrument back, when I looked at it closely, I abandoned that project. Music can always come in handy. When I dusted off the bagpipe, when I adjusted it, I managed to get a few sounds out of it, but I stopped right away. The walls of this room are like cardboard and someone had started pounding in the room next door.

Victor Daguerre's chalet keeps running through my head, too. Marthe wasn't very enthusiastic at first, but after I told her about the incident in Oakland she wanted to go there with me. I'm not sure what to think. If the place is the hovel she described, I could probably find something better. But there it is. Shut up in this motel room I'm not going anywhere, I'm not making any decisions. I'm in mourning.

Also, Barnum owes me money. I keep expecting a cheque every day. With what I've saved over the years it will be easier to make a decision. No, I won't go to the lake. Or maybe some other time. I won't budge from here until this matter has been settled.

... and then I remembered that Marthe used to play the piano. Her mother was the one who urged her to take lessons. She had a certain talent. I thought about it again as I looked at the flute in its case. At Marthe's place, in her house, we could play without disturbing anyone. Maybe she'd be interested.

Chapter 4
The Music

There were three children at the gate to the house. Hugo stopped in front of them, opened the case and took out the instrument. He gesticulated like a mime and the children were fascinated. One of them asked if they had to pay for the show. Hugo shook his head and showed them the strange flute with its sympathetic cords and its mouthpiece that covered both nose and mouth. Two breathing-holes had been pierced at the nostrils.

He covered his mouth with this thing that looked like a gas mask and began to speak. In the circus, with the elephant, the costume and the makeup, the effect had been flamboyant. Now, without the animal, he felt slightly naked. But he couldn't help it, he needed to put on a show.

It had been going on for barely five minutes when he spotted Marthe at the end of the street. He hadn't phoned before coming and suddenly he was afraid of annoying her. The music stopped then and there.

"No, no, don't stop! That was beautiful!"

Marthe's hair was no longer in a bun and she was

holding something in her hands, a bottle most likely.

"I ... I was in the neighbourhood. I wanted to say goodbye before I left."

"Oh — are you going away?"

Hugo quickly put the instrument away and Marthe didn't even try to hide her disappointment. He always looked hunted, this half-brother of hers, as if someone were after him. Maybe he was trying to impress her. Nonchalantly, she took a bunch of keys from her purse and turned towards the gate.

"Did your suitcase ever turn up?"

He shook his head. She opened the gate and they went into the garden. The children, disappointed, clung to the iron bars of the gate and watched them.

"I was expecting to hear from you. About, you know, going up to the lake...."

"I've thought about it. But not now ... not right away."

She climbed the few steps to the veranda and opened the door. Before going inside, Hugo took a last look at the street. They were still there, waiting for him, and he waved at them.

Inside, Marthe immediately went into the living-room, put her things on the table covered with books, then came back to him. The instrument had aroused her curiosity. She wanted a closer look so Hugo lifted the cover.

"Where on earth did you dig that up? I've never seen a set of bagpipes like that."

"It was from Sally. Barnum and Bailey made it. You just talk into it and it makes sounds. It's for the parade mainly — for the opening act."

"The parade?"

"It makes a noise. It's very colourful."

Marthe turned the instrument over and over and touched the keys, all the while looking into Hugo's eyes. She was about to bring it to her mouth, but stopped in mid-movement.

"Since you're going away, we'll have to drink a toast!"

She returned the instrument to its case, opened the bag she'd set on the table and took out a bottle. Radiant, Marthe beckoned him to follow her, pointing to the main staircase.

"Come on. It's more comfortable upstairs. It was my parents' bedroom, the biggest one in the house. After Mama died I moved in there. I fixed it up as an apartment for myself. It's very pleasant."

Hugo, who was following her, stopped at the top of the stairs. Books were everywhere: spilling out of cupboards and closets, piled in the hallway, rising to the ceiling in piles big and small. There were paths between these blocks of books, boulevards leading to a bedroom at the very back. Hugo was interested, but she grabbed his arm and led him in the opposite direction.

The apartment she had told him about was completely unlike the rest of the house. Even the light was different there. Perhaps it was because of the window that looked out on the alley, or the makeup table with its semicircle of lightbulbs. He immediately thought of Sally, of Sally's dressing-room.

"You know, after you left the other day I went looking for you. I wanted so much to tell you how I felt."

She was opening the bottle as she spoke; her movements were brusque and she was awkward. He took the corkscrew from her hands. It was a bottle of Cahors. In just a few days Marthe had been transformed. She looked nothing at all like the dull librarian he'd met on that first day. Her dramatic little manner had faded away.

She was rather feverish.

"Would you like to taste it?"

"No, you go ahead!"

He pretended to be interested in the label while she looked for another glass. He swore that he didn't know a thing about wine and that in his opinion there were just two kinds: good and bad. They tasted it together and decided that this one wasn't bad.

"If you weren't so busy we could have a little outing next week."

"Do you mean to the chalet?"

She suppressed a smile and led him to a brighter corner of this big room that had once been Victor Daguerre's bedroom. Farther away was a double bed and, near the window, a big Chinese chest of drawers. On the left, a kitchenette with a sink, stove and refrigerator. It was like a house within a house, and it was a much warmer place than any of the rooms on the main floor. Marthe took two sips of wine, then mounted a fresh offensive.

"You know, the chalet may not be in such bad shape. My memories are, though. I'd be prepared to go up any time, as long as it's not a Saturday or Sunday."

She asked the questions and she supplied the answers. She was talking to herself as she turned her glass before her eyes, and all Hugo did was nod.

"Papa was very attached to that plot of land. He bought it in 1964, the year I was born."

"The year he left my mother," Hugo added.

She frowned, took a big sip of wine and went on as if he hadn't spoken.

"We used to spend our summers up there. Papa closed the bookstore and took up piles of books, so he wouldn't lose his touch. He was always on the veranda, he'd stay there all day long, reading three books at once. The wrinkles would disappear from his face, the tone of his voice changed. He'd become attentive again. In the evening, he'd talk to us about Asia, Egypt — all the countries he'd visited that day, which he'd spin into a sort of travelogue for us. And Mama and I would listen to him for hours. He'd get lost in the details, take the most amazing detours. If you listened to him, the world could fit in a handkerchief. He'd talk about Cleopatra and Napoleon as if he'd known them. He knew so much that, before I fell asleep, I'd ask my mother where he'd learned it all. Her answer was always the same: 'Your father has read everything. And he remembers things that haven't even been written yet.'"

Marthe's eyes were sparkling. Hugo put down his glass and scrutinized her face at length. She was ravishing and full of energy. He wondered how he could have hesitated all this time, how he could have spent the week in his motel and not got in touch with her. This was the best thing that had happened to him since Chicago.

"It seems to me that everything was white back then. My mother and I wore white dresses, Papa a Panama hat and loose linen trousers. We'd spend whole afternoons washing and hanging up clothes. Cleanliness was a daily activity. We used to talk about it, comment on it. That's all there was at Lake St. Francis: my father's books and all that whiteness."

Hugo poured more wine for her and ventured to ask a new question:

"Was that before the picnics in the park? Before you and I tore each other apart to get his attention?"

"Long before that. I was seven or eight. I still thought I was an only child. I mean, so to speak."

Hugo merely smiled. It was very good that she was

talking like this. He'd said too much at their first meeting, bared his soul to her. That must have been why he'd hesitated before coming back.

"There was a farmer who lived on the shore of the lake. In the summer he raised animals, in the winter he cut wood. It was from him that my father bought the land. He had a son, Germain, who was much too big for his age. A huge little giant who never knew what to do with his body. Germain had no ambitions, except maybe to look after his father's animals when he was even bigger.

"Some days our clothes were so white and there was so little to do that my father would send me over to play with Germain. We'd sit on a log by the lake, Germain and I, and throw pebbles into the water. From across the lake we could see a column of smoke rising into the air. 'That's the Indian campground,' Germain told me. And for the rest of the day he'd terrify me by telling me how the Indians tortured and scalped and ate their victims.

"Then one day I'd had enough. I thought he was so boring. I took the path back to the house. My father wasn't on the veranda. His book was on the table and the pages were turning in the breeze. Only half the clothes were on the line and there wasn't a sound inside the cottage. I went to the window that looked into their bedroom. My father and my mother were lying on the bed and talking. About that other woman ... and her child. That was the first time I ever heard about you. And do you know what I did then? I cried. I started to cry and yell and say that Germain had hurt me. My father came out right away. He'd put on a bathrobe that wasn't really closed. He smelled of sweat, he was all worked up, and he touched me to see where I hurt. I still remember his smell. The smell of a man. When he put his arms around me I wished I could stay there for the rest of my life, nestled up against him.... And I think he felt the same thing."

She had taken that detour, told him about the big little giant and the Indians who massacred their victims, in order to arrive at this point. At this very precise, very clear memory of desire. Victor Daguerre was drifting in her gaze, as real there as he was absent from Hugo's life. It was a kind of confession, an indiscretion that wasn't one. He had always known that his half-sister and his father loved each other. He simply hadn't known the details of that love.

"The reason I've read all my life, the reason I still read, is that I've never stopped looking for him! The books were where he lived. Even today, when I turn the pages of a book, I have the impression that he's there, that he's going to show up. The past and the present run together. Between two chapters I'll find his odour, a dog-eared page, a wild-rose leaf marking a passage. And when I read I have the impression that I'm stirred in the same places he was."

Hugo was irritated. There was something menacing about this little film that Marthe was unreeling. He preferred to hate Victor Daguerre. Not to know there was something appealing about him. With a gloomy look he drained his glass and turned his head slightly, as if this story didn't interest him any more.

"And what about Germain?" he asked, cool now. "What happened to him?"

Marthe was disappointed, but she tried not to show it. Hugo's indifference had taken the wind out of her sails. Had he not interrupted her like this, she'd have gone on talking about Victor Daguerre for another hour. She would have got to the bottom of the story the way one touches the bottom of a barrel. For once, she would have told everything. But perhaps the time wasn't right yet.

"Germain? I saw him again about ten years ago. But I couldn't talk to him. He's seven feet tall — a genuine giant. And he still doesn't know what to do with his body."

Hugo held back a smile. He was quite fond of giants. There are always giants in the circus. And it beat talking about Victor Daguerre.

*

A little later they came back downstairs. Marthe wanted to take a closer look at the musical instrument. To touch it, try it out. The two of them bent over the case and Hugo explained how it worked. Words, spoken clearly into the mouthpiece, activated a system of reeds concealed by a small wooden cover. Through sympathetic vibration, violin strings attached to the top would produce the sound of wind or waves, depending on how it was played.

"Does this gas mask of yours have a name?"

Sally and Bobby had simply called it "the flute." Apparently it was a reproduction of an old instrument. One that the gypsies used to carry around with them. It had been reconstructed from sketches and memories.

"It's simple, you just have to talk into it!"

Marthe brought the instrument to her mouth. The mask covered part of her face. She was not really comfortable, and it took two tries before she produced a sound: a muffled bleat that sounded like the cry of a seal on an ice floe. Laughter. They were like two children with a new toy.

"Try again!"

This time the "flute" whined on the high notes and Hugo clapped his hands over his ears.

"You don't have to yell."

"I know, I know. You just talk."

It was the wine — and the atmosphere, which was growing more and more relaxed. Taking a deep breath, she closed her eyes and whispered very softly. And then a melody spread through the house, something very soft, suggestive of a violin but more fluid. She played the passage a second time, then a third, twisting the notes and smoothing their angles.

"That's wonderful!" said Hugo. "When I blow into it, it just makes noise."

There was something mellow about the inflection Marthe gave the words, yet she was barely murmuring into the mask.

"What are you saying? What are the words?"

"Nothing special — whatever comes into my head."

"And what comes into your head?"

Instead of replying, she turned her back and continued to play, making her way towards the living-room. Despite a few snags, there was mastery in her playing, a finesse he had never before heard emerging from this jumble of pipes. When she entered the room the echo joined the music, producing harmonies that were even more delightful.

The more she spoke into the instrument, the more Hugo was convinced that she was declaiming some great masterpiece taken from her father's books. He had never heard anything like it.

Now she was standing near the sofa. She had fallen

silent and, even from a distance, he knew she was uncomfortable. It was his compliment, perhaps, or the music that had come out spontaneously, that had in a sense undressed her.

"No, no. Don't stop. Keep playing."

She touched the instrument's keys and placed her fingers over each of the holes. She was trying to comprehend the logic of the mechanism, while imagining all the music hidden in these pipes.

Then Hugo pictured her under the big top, holding the instrument, making sublime music while he played the clown around her — like Bobby and his niece, Sally. Marthe was still weighing the instrument in her hands, listening to the sound of it, pinching its cords or stroking them with her damp hands.

"If it were up to me, I'd call it the Lexiphone. Since you just have to talk into it, it makes sense, I think."

"The Lexiphone?"

She chortled. Hugo wasn't sure he understood, wasn't sure he found it as funny as she did, but he put his arm around her.

It was a slow and affectionate gesture. The last time he had done this, it had been with Sally, in the dressing-room, before the show in Oakland. And he thought again about the odour of men ... the odour of Victor Daguerre. Why had she told him that story? And why had he interrupted her? What had she tried to tell him that he didn't want to hear?

He was holding her tight, but he didn't dare look at her too closely. This sudden familiarity made them both nervous. Marthe brought the instrument to her mouth. And what she said into the Lexiphone must have been very beautiful, because the music was sublime.

Chapter 5
The Clown

Before departing Chicago I left an address and a Florida bank account number. The money from Barnum is supposed to be deposited there. But the transfer is taking ages. I stay by the phone and the days drag on and on. For a while I thought I'd feel comfortable in this room ... for ever. At the moment, though, I'm not so sure.

Since our second meeting, Marthe has called at least three times. She would like me to move to Éliane Street, but for the time being that's out of the question. There's something about her I can't quite put my finger on. Some days, it's the light. Other days, the shadow. I have the impression that she's fragile, a dam about to burst. If I push, the floodgates will open. And I'll be submerged. I don't know if I could live with that. To come to terms with her mysteries while I make my way back to the circus. Things with Sally and Bobby may have been crazy, but they were basically a lot simpler.

When I arrived in Montreal, in that train station I took for a big top, I was the ringmaster, the one who made the show happen. Now, I'm once again what I've always been: a clown. Except that my suitcase has disappeared, my costume and all the props I need for my work have vanished into thin air. I'm a buffoon but it doesn't show. Actually, it may be better that way. I'm not trying to be someone else.

I'm a little more like the Hugo Daguerre who ran away to the United States ten years ago. At the time I was falling apart. Nobody wanted to see me, nobody wanted me at all. The wound was still fresh and it could have been healed. But since then I've made it my *raison d'être*. It has become my profession, and the wound is a gaping hole. In the circus there were never enough spotlights or faces or applause to fill that gulf. I would have sold my soul to make people laugh, to make them love me, to be somebody.

The more I think about Bobby, and the more I think about his rage, the more my fear fades away. Distance is part of it, of course, but there's something else too. I bet that, like me, he dreams about the circus, that he wants to put on an act, wants to go back to the footlights. Once you've tasted that, there's nothing else! But he will never find another target as captivating as Sally. Like me he's in the wings, waiting to go on.

There's one good thing about my retreat into the room at the back of the Motel Émard. I've thought it over and I know there won't be a knife-thrower in my circus. Too dangerous. Instead, there will be music, fantasy, magic even. When Marthe began to play the other day, it was luminous. I could feel it in my guts: a pinch, a tightening. Something had just appeared, something that hadn't been there three seconds earlier. She's fascinating, my half-sister, with her age that is constantly changing, her sense of the dramatic and her music. I'll go to see her again.

*

Marthe just called. I was dozing and stroking the silky pages of the book when the phone wakened me. I still haven't read a single poem by Baudelaire. I'm content to touch them with my fingertips. I'm the physical type, in any case. With Victor Daguerre everything was in the mind, it was cerebral, and to take my revenge I'm making Baudelaire wait.

Marthe has just called. At first I thought it was the bank, and I had trouble hiding my disappointment. She realized that, but she didn't let it show. On the contrary, she made a proposal: she had several days off the following week and she'd like to go to the lake.

"You come too," she said. "It will do you good. And you can meet Germain."

I think it was the giant who made the difference. A foretaste of the circus. I agreed to go.

"Would you mind bringing the Lexiphone?" she asked. "I'd love to try playing it outdoors."

"No problem!"

We settled on a time and a day in the middle of the week. The more I think about it, the more I think we should have made this trip before.

Chapter 6
The Giant, Baudelaire and Grass

The bus to Lake St. Francis was packed that day. Hugo and Marthe were in the very back seat, watching the noisy crowd pointing and squawking. It was a far cry from the shuttle that had made the trip in the past. This was a subway car that had lost its way in an endless suburb.

Hugo had stowed the Lexiphone's case under the seat and he was holding a wicker basket on his lap. The city stretched out endlessly, the countryside was more and more remote, and Marthe was not really surprised at what she was seeing. When the driver stopped the vehicle along the road and announced: "Lake St. Francis!" she made a face as if a verdict had just been declared. She went up the aisle of the bus, followed by Hugo, who was trying to see the lake through the windows. The doors opened and the driver muttered something that sounded vaguely like:

"Mynah the step!"

They found themselves standing on the highway, facing a winding road that disappeared into the undergrowth. It was drizzling slightly and Marthe observed, disappointed:

"This is pretty well what I was expecting!"

Hugo, on the lookout, peered all round him, seeking some sign, some reminder of what this place had been like fifteen years before. On the other side of the road there was a new city. A jigsaw of condos and low-cost housing that surrounded the undergrowth and the lake.

"Come on, it must be better near the water," he exclaimed in a tone of false enthusiasm.

Everything was grey, the rain was coming down harder, and Hugo picked up the basket decisively. Marthe hung onto the Lexiphone and they started down the road.

"I don't recognize a thing. It's all changed."

Between the stunted trees they spied dozens of chalets elbowing one another at the water's edge: small boxes with no charm, half rotted, piled up on top of one another like the travellers on the bus.

"We won't spend the night here. I bet we'll be off again in half an hour."

"I'd like to take a look anyway. Surely there's something left."

They walked through the undergrowth for a while, along the paths between the cabins. They didn't see a soul; not the slightest sign of life in this summertime shantytown.

"Let's not stay," Marthe said again. "I had some good memories, I'd like to keep them intact."

Just then a woman materialized out of nowhere. She was stately-looking and she had coarse features. Her dishevelled hair stood up on her head in an intriguing disorder. Bending over to Marthe she murmured:

"My sister, my child...."

"I beg your pardon!"

Her familiarity had made Marthe shrink back. Perhaps it was the choice of words. Their resonance. The woman stood at least two heads taller than them and she was literally blocking the path.

"We're looking for Victor Daguerre's chalet," said Hugo. "Do you know where it is?"

At that, a half-smile appeared on her face. The coarseness of her features diminished somewhat and she nodded.

"You know the Daguerres?"

Marthe nodded. Hugo followed suit and the woman began to laugh. A laugh that was guttural, nearly lewd. It was apparent that alcohol had something to do with it. Alcohol that had left its marks.

"This will make Germain so happy," she whispered, revealing two broad rows of teeth.

"Oh, do you know Germain?"

Now her laughter became conspiratorial.

"Oh yes. He looks after the horses. He has a riding school and he takes summer people riding."

"So the chalet's still there?" Hugo asked.

"Absolutely. Come, I'll show you."

Without further ado, the inordinately tall woman turned on her heel and led the way. Marthe and Hugo followed behind her, but she completely blocked their view of the scenery. Her shoulders formed a veritable screen, and with every step she took her feet sank deeply into the pine needles. They walked down towards the shore, then turned right. On the path skirting the lake, she spoke again.

"In July there are lots of people here. But off season you have to keep an eye on things. There've been robberies...."

That explained the rather chilly welcome. Her build

made her a very good security guard, but the longer they walked, the more relaxed the atmosphere became. At one point she turned to Marthe.

"You're the bookseller's daughter, I assume?"

The two women shook hands and the giantess announced:

"My name's Gaël. I've been living here for a few years now...."

Hugo introduced himself as well, without going into details about his status or the reason for their visit. He'd taken a liking to this woman who, under a graceless exterior, was actually very warm.

"You know, Germain went on looking after the chalet. He always thought somebody would come back some day...."

Hugo was delighted to hear it. Those words were meant for him. It was written in the sky some place. One of the Daguerres would need the chalet some day, and it would be there waiting.

At a bend in the path, Marthe stopped abruptly. She had spotted the little house. The weather had had its way with the paint, there was greenish moss on part of the roof, but it was still magnificent. A place for contemplation in the middle of this pine grove dotted with cabins.

Marthe went up to the veranda where her father had spent so many hours reading. The screen was battered, in several places the floor had given way, but it was still there. The chalet of her childhood. And yet, when Hugo asked her if she recognized the spot, she shook her head.

"It's all changed so much, I'm not sure...."

But she was lying. Hugo knew it. Gaël too, for that matter. Suppressing a smile, she opened the door.

The white was far less white than it had once been,

the chalet was even smaller than she'd imagined, but it was all there. Very basic furniture, a sofa, a table, some chairs.... The place was clean and the odour suggested that it was inhabited.

Holding the Lexiphone against her chest, Marthe slowly advanced. Her head was thrown back, as if she feared a blow. Stopping at the big window, the one that looked out on the lake, she gazed at the horizon. Behind her, Hugo was opening all the doors, all the closets. He peered into the bedrooms, into every nook and cranny. Gaël too felt at home here. From the cupboard under the sink she had taken a container of water; then she reached out her arm and took down three cups from the shelf.

Hugo returned to the table and took a seat there, totally at ease. There was something reminiscent of Brueghel in the sight of Gaël's imposing silhouette bent over the stove. The aroma of tea began to spread through the little house. Marthe still had her back to them. She didn't know what to make of this woman who was probably squatting here. A tramp who had found in Germain a man who was a match for her. She could think of only one thing — to get out of here as quickly as possible — whereas Hugo was beginning to take root.

"Have you known Germain very long?"

Gaël started laughing again. The same husky growl.

"When he sees smoke from the chimney he usually drops in...."

She talked about it as if it were a lovers' tryst. About the smoke from the chimney as a kind of invitation. Something sparkled in her gaze and it was obvious to Hugo that the woman was in love.

While she was pouring the tea, Hugo took an interest in the structure of the house. In his opinion the house was still solid. It could last for years.

"The lake, on the other hand, is disappointing ... I mean ... the uncontrolled development around it."

Gaël set a cup in front of Hugo, agreeing with him that it must have been wonderful here at one time.

Marthe was in a trance, a kind of numbness. She politely refused the cup of tea she'd been offered. Retreating, Gaël set the cup on the table, then turned to put a log in the stove.

Marthe's attitude left Gaël deeply perplexed. Pushing back a lock of hair that had fallen onto her forehead, she turned towards Hugo.

"Is anything wrong?"

Nodding, he turned towards his half-sister and murmured:

"An old sadness."

Hugo had accompanied these words with a wave of his hand, as if to minimize their impact. Gaël's face became unattractive again. Or was she feeling pain? Her broad shoulders were slumped and she seemed to be trying to find a solution to the situation.

If Marthe had taken to her heels no one would have been surprised. The atmosphere was heavy enough to cut with a knife. But it was Gaël who withdrew to one of the bedrooms.

Hugo sipped his tea. He respected his half-sister's silence and adapted to the situation as best he could.

As soon as he'd finished his tea, as soon as that woman came back, they would say their goodbyes and be on their way.

Marthe remained as tense as ever. Gaël stayed in the bedroom for long minutes and Hugo poured himself another cup of tea. When Gaël emerged she was holding a pipe. She stuffed it with tobacco with her thumb, then looked around the stove for matches. Looking down from

her great height, she declaimed:
"To move away from sorrow's shores."
Marthe started, as she had done on the path a little earlier.

"What did you say?"

Gaël was smiling broadly, but she didn't reply. When she cracked the match, an acrid odour spread through the chalet. Marthe was staring insistently at her when she added:

"Your eyes reflect the sunset and the dawn;
you scatter perfumes like a windy night."

It was stupefying. Gaël's tone and delivery were perfect. Not only was she inspired when she recited the words, it seemed as if she'd written them herself. A celestial tramp!

Marthe took the pipe Gaël offered her as if it was the obvious thing to do. She who never smoked, she the level-headed librarian, took a long drag on the peace-pipe without asking any questions.

Gaël appeared relieved. So this melancholy young woman standing at the window didn't turn down every gift she was offered. Gaël took back the pipe and turned towards Hugo, who smoked as well. The smell of grass spread its wings. This odd tobacco clouded their minds and no one was sure about what was being said, what was really going on. Was the woman with the hair of a *poète maudit* speaking in stanzas, or was it an illusion? What erudition had all at once struck this giantess? The bluish smoke swept across their faces; Marthe was still clutching the Lexiphone and she wondered whether Baudelaire's words had been uttered before or after they'd smoked.

She set the case down at her feet and looked out at the veranda. She had an urge to go outside, to see it from closer range. The floor creaked under her feet. Gaël had gone back to sit across from Hugo. She was all smiles and continued to drag on the pipe. As soon as Marthe had stepped outside, a voice behind her scolded:

"Where've you been?"

She turned towards the wicker chair and opened her mouth, but the words were stuck.

"I ... umm ... next door, at Germain's."

Marthe's voice was the voice of her childhood. A nasal, musical little voice, even when it wasn't appropriate. She gave him a little nod. The bookseller nodded back. Victor Daguerre was wearing the same linen pants ... the same Panama hat.

"I've been wanting to talk to you for quite a while now," she mumbled.

"Don't tell me you want to go over all that again!"

She shrank back, tried to pull herself together, then spat out, annoyed:

"You always say that! But we never actually talk about it! It weighs on my heart, you know."

"That was so long ago. It's in the past. Be reasonable...."

"I have been reasonable. But now I don't feel like it any more!"

Old Daguerre closed his book. He no longer recognized his little Marthe. She was arrogant, vindictive even. He tried to calm her.

"You've been lucky in life. You're educated, you have all the books, the house, a job you like...."

"Papa, I want to settle this once and for all."

Her tone was increasingly febrile. Again the bookseller tried to dodge the subject.

"Why dig up the dead? You're only hurting yourself, Marthe."

"But I am hurting!"

"Look, it happened once or twice."

"Five times, Papa. Five times!"

"All right, maybe five times, but I didn't want to hurt you. And remember how things were. Your mother was very sick. We were distraught."

The old man was trembling. He was having more and more trouble finding his words, while Marthe was looking daggers at him.

"Maybe you'd like me to get down on my knees?" he suggested with a hint of sarcasm.

"You really don't understand a thing, Papa! It's a heavy burden to bear. I want us to have it out once and for all!"

"It's unfortunate ... but what do you want me to say, it happened! We had relations ... what else can I say?"

"That's it! I wanted to hear you say it!"

"But it was years ago. It just happened — that's all!"

Victor Daguerre was exasperated. He pounded on his book to mark each word. Saliva was dribbling from both sides of his mouth, but Marthe was unruffled. For years she had been preparing herself for this encounter and she wasn't going to back off now.

"But I'm your daughter, Papa!"

"Ah! And that's what you want to hear me say. You want me to play the good daddy and tell you, 'Yes, my darling daughter.' But you aren't my daughter. In fact that's why this business happened. Which is no excuse, but...."

He bit his lip in mid-sentence. An awkward pause settled between them and for a long moment they stayed as they were, silent. The bookseller was all shrivelled up. He felt ashamed, and he played with the turned-down corner of a page in his book while he waited for her to say something, to forgive him, perhaps. But that was the last thing she intended to do. Instead, she savoured the moment as a victory, as if he had finally come clean.

A door creaked behind her. Germain, the farmer's son, entered the house with outstretched hand. He was impressive — a colossus whose head touched the beams in the ceiling. Hugo was thrilled. And so, obviously, was Gaël. She had come up to him, she was stroking his hand, and her eyes had become prisms. Proportions notwithstanding, they were a handsome little couple.

"Poor Marthe," mumbled the old bookseller on the veranda. "If you only knew how sorry I am."

He was sincere. He was holding his head in both hands and seemed to be in despair. In fact, she might have taken pity on him had he not added:

"If you don't mind ... I'd like to keep this matter just between us. I'd rather you didn't tell anybody."

"Why?"

"It's just so unfortunate."

She came back to him, tried to grab his shoulders and shake him, but when she reached out there was nothing there. Instinctively she turned back towards the chalet, where Germain and Hugo were talking louder and louder. She wanted to beckon them to come and listen too. But she didn't dare. Victor Daguerre had been dead for a long time. They wouldn't believe her.

Giving up the battle, she opened the door and came back inside. A strange confusion reigned inside the chalet. Maybe it was the grass, maybe it was the circus. An impassioned conversation was under way. Something about big tops and trained animals.

Marthe lingered in the doorway briefly. She was fascinated by Gaël and Germain, by the body language that brought them close together. When one spoke, the other vibrated. They held hands discreetly and swayed to the same rhythm. Gaël was in no way beautiful,

Germain's disproportion was close to outrageous, yet together they were a beautiful sight. A couple in love.

Germain noticed her first. He turned towards her, the conversation broke off abruptly, and he flung open his arms. As had happened the last time they'd met, Marthe felt suddenly dizzy. The giant was coming nearer. He was about to take her in his arms ... when the floor gave way under her feet.

Gaël, who had seen it coming, shoved the two men aside to catch her as she fell. All at once Marthe found herself in the other woman's comfortable arms, and she started to cry. Torrents ran down her cheeks; she sniffled like a child, and wondered what was happening to her.

"When a person knows she's right," Gaël murmured, "she doesn't try to convince those who are wrong."

The words hit her like a punch and the storm stopped right away. Marthe swallowed her sorrow and stared at Gaël once again. She peered at this woman who had scared her at first, this woman who had led her into the maze of grass and who knew what had happened on the veranda.

"Do you feel better now?" she asked.

Gently Marthe freed herself from her embrace and nodded. Then the giantess walked out of the house, waving her arms above her head. Gaël was chasing away the bookseller just as you chase away dogs that come prowling at night. The woman was truly a witch. She knew how to talk to the dead ... and even more, how to scare them.

Still wobbly, Marthe turned towards Hugo, who offered her his shoulder. A week ago he wouldn't have tolerated such intimacy, such intensity. He'd have wriggled out of it, tried to find some excuse. This time, though, he did nothing of the kind. She could cry all the tears in her body and he wouldn't push her away.

Chapter 7
Sets

It was very hot when they got back to the city. Summer had arrived all at once and, as soon as they were inside the house, Marthe closed the shutters and drew the curtains. She was not very talkative and she soon retired to her apartment. The night at Lake St. Francis had exhausted her. She needed to stop for a while, to think it all over.

Hugo made himself very discreet. As the weather was unbearable he decided to take a nap before going back to the motel. Unlike his sister, he was delighted by the trip to the lake. Germain the giant had a passion for animals, and as soon as Hugo mentioned the circus they'd become bosom buddies. Maybe they'd work together some day.

After he had cleaned out the picnic basket and put away the Lexiphone, he went into the living-room and flopped onto the sofa. Alone in the midst of his father's books. Alone in this intimidating house that he was just starting to get to know. The trip to the lake had brought him closer to Marthe. When she'd burst into tears and come to cry on his shoulder, he had spent an hour consoling her, without asking why she was crying. He loved her — he owed her that much.

For the rest of the day, Hugo dozed on the sofa while he thought about what lay ahead. The money from Barnum's that might not arrive, his suitcase and various objects that seemed to have disappeared for good. Several hours passed that way. The sultriness of the day dissipated, and when he opened his eyes late in the afternoon Marthe was standing on the stairs. Her tremendous fatigue seemed to have vanished. In fact, she had the air of being up to something.

Marthe headed for a closet and opened it with a lot of crashing and banging. She took out a carton and dropped it in the middle of the room. In a sudden frenzy, she threw herself on the books, on the piles of volumes that were taking over the ground floor of the house. She flung them into the box by the armful. She demolished the skyscrapers, wiped out the boulevards of the miniature cities. Nothing could slow her down, and as soon as the first box was empty she went to the basement to look for more. Still drowsy, Hugo followed these goings-on and couldn't help saying:

"Is that it? Are the excavations finished? Are you putting your father away?"

Nodding vaguely, she went on flinging books into boxes. Amused, he sat up to get some sense of the scope of the exercise. There was enough to fill a good thirty cartons. On her own, it would take his half-sister two days.

"And that's not all," she announced, stopping in the midst of this major cleanup. "I'm quitting my job at the library. I've had enough. It's over, that's it!"

Marthe was out of control. The first time he'd seen her he'd never have thought her capable of such a transformation. He had thought she'd be a librarian for ever.

"I turn thirty this August. I've had it! It's time to move on to something else."

Now nothing could stop her. The piles of books were melting before his eyes. Already the mini-architecture that had so intrigued Hugo on his arrival had ceased to exist. This was a fury. The pile of cartons in the entrance formed an effective barricade. The set was being rapidly transformed and a big piece of furniture was revealed in the middle of the living-room. One whose presence Hugo hadn't even suspected. It was a black-and-white television fitted into a cabinet that also housed a stereo system. A monster of polished wood with a Garrard turntable and concealed speakers.

"Does this work?" he asked, stroking the old set.

"I don't know. Maybe. It's been there for years."

Marthe had no time to talk. No time to explain. Urgency showed in every move she made, and little by little the curtain was rising on this set from another time: forgotten knick-knacks, lamps that appeared out of nowhere. A window blocked by a wall of books. It was a tornado, a tidal wave ... nothing was safe from it!

An hour later Hugo had already lugged fifteen cartons upstairs. He suggested putting them in the closed room at the end of the corridor, but she refused categorically so he stowed them along one wall, leaving enough room to pass. Every time he went down to the living-room, he stopped in front of the TV set for a closer look. It was a model with doors that closed over the screen. As he was trying to open them, Marthe asked him to give her a hand; one of the cartons was heavier than the others and she couldn't move it.

The hurricane raged until early evening. Then, when Victor Daguerre's books had completely disappeared,

Marthe let herself collapse onto the sofa with an expression of relief. The big cabinet that housed the TV set now sat naked in the middle of the room. Hugo jabbered something about the Motel Émard, while she seemed amazed at the size of the living-room.

"Just shifting a few pieces of furniture would make this room look totally different."

"If we had the strength to do it."

Taking his remark as a challenge, she got up, more energetic than ever. In a renewed tempest which lasted for another good hour, they moved everything that came to hand. The big sofa, the armchairs and tables. Everything waltzed across the room, as if Marthe were waging all-out war. The sofa ended up in front of the old TV set, with a low table between them. An island in the middle of this big living-room. All the other furniture had been placed along the wall.

When Marthe threw in the towel, they both collapsed onto the sofa and stayed there without moving for a long moment, saying nothing, their souls at rest.

"You know what struck me yesterday at the lake?" she admitted a minute later.

Hugo grunted vaguely. He was falling asleep. She rose discreetly and took a few steps towards the bathroom.

"... what struck you?"

His eyes were heavy. She had stopped and seemed to be searching for words.

"Gaël and Germain. You know, the way they held hands ... and looked at each other."

"Yes, I think they're happy together."

"Love among the giants," she murmured. "I hadn't thought about it before.... You just need to find a kindred spirit, I suppose."

Hugo had straightened up. Her expression was vague.

He wished she would come back, wished they could talk for a while longer. All she added was:

"You can sleep there if you want. It will be hot at your motel. You'll be more comfortable here."

Her voice was quavering slightly. Perhaps she didn't want to be alone? The house had changed so much. Maybe she needed a presence, someone to reassure her when she woke up the next morning.

"All right, if you like. Your sofa's very comfortable."

She nodded quickly and disappeared behind the bathroom door. Hugo had agreed without thinking, but it was all the same to him. Whether he slept in his motel room or in this big empty living-room, what was the difference?

Instinctively he turned to the TV set and started fiddling with all the knobs at once. A bluish glow came from the screen, something like a picture awash in thick fog. Hugo turned off the set, then turned it on and tried one last adjustment, but he was unable to get anything like a picture from the set. Blue calm.

He let his gaze travel around the big room, then farther away, to the front hall. Without thinking about it any more, he got up and went all over the main floor, switching off lights. Back on the sofa, he admired the results. The blue glow from the TV set now illuminated the whole room, the whole floor even. The austerity was gone. The high ceilings drank up the light. Only a glimmer of it remained.

It was a good half-hour before Marthe emerged from the bathroom, swaddled in her bathrobe. She was surprised at the change in the lighting, but she had something else on her mind: to get the Lexiphone from the dining-room. Hugging the instrument in her arms, she came back to the sofa.

"There's something else I wanted to ask you. Yesterday at the lake ... I don't really remember too well ... was it before we smoked that grass or after that Gaël started talking like Baudelaire? I mean, quoting the poetry?"

He shrugged and turned back to the blue glow to hide his embarrassment.

"Baudelaire? I don't remember her talking about Baudelaire. I think it's her style, that's the way she is ... it's just the way she talks."

Marthe didn't believe this and sat there for a long moment, leaning against the back of the sofa, her mind elsewhere, her gaze uncertain. Hugo would have turned around, would have looked her straight in the eye, but something stopped him. The scent of soap or cream floating around them. A memory. Sally, maybe. If he hadn't restrained himself he would have kissed her on the cheek. Instead he asked:

"Do you really think there are no more pictures in this TV?"

"Probably not. It must be all emptied out," she replied.

She dashed towards the staircase. Marthe wasn't walking now, she was levitating. She floated above the steps, but when Hugo turned around she had disappeared.

Accepting her invitation had been an excellent idea. He hadn't felt this good for a long time.

Chapter 8
Ghosts

For half an hour now Marthe has been playing the Lexiphone upstairs. A perfume is spreading through the house, her music touches me very deeply, and if I followed my instinct I'd go up there so I could hear it better. Who'd have thought you could get such beautiful sounds from those bagpipes? I wonder just what she's saying.

At the Motel Émard I didn't have a TV set. Only a view of the park. In a way, Victor Daguerre's living-room is a significant improvement. The blue glow and Marthe's music. Bliss.

There's been a genuine revolution in this house today. Some of those books had been there for twenty years. The change is so radical that the house seems a little naked, nearly empty. It reminds me of the circus. Behind one set there is always another one. And the quicker the changes, the more dazzling the effect. The bookseller himself couldn't find his way around here. But what surprised me most was Marthe's anger in the midst of all these upheavals. As if she wanted to erase something, forget it at all costs, cancel it, though there aren't just bad things in her father's books. I'm in no position to say this, but personally I thought Baudelaire was pretty good.

Wait a minute! She's just stopped. A while ago she couldn't even stand up. And it's just as well that she's going to sleep before I do. On my first night in her house I'd rather stay awake for a while, keep an eye on the scenery. I've made myself a nest in the sofa and I've rolled the blanket into a ball, as if I were holding Sally against me. Sounds are coming from the kitchen ... or from farther away, from the lane. My eyes are heavier and heavier, but I can't get to sleep.

Either I'm dreaming or somebody's forcing a door. There was a little knocking sound just now, at the other end of the house. A door or a window, I don't know which. All at once I'm in the middle of the living-room, standing there with my arms held out. I know perfectly well it's ridiculous, but I have the feeling someone has just come in. I can hear footsteps. I have to stay calm. It may be nothing, but I'd just as soon see for myself.

The ground floor is even bigger than I'd pictured it. The pantry is the size of a garage, and under the main staircase there's a black hole. The lane is deserted and I'm alone as I stroll through the house, looking for ghosts. I'm thinking of Victor Daguerre, of course. He must be the one prowling here, he must be looking for his books. Unless he's come to chase me away.

I go back to the sofa, my island in the middle of the living-room, and clutch at the blue glow from the television. Victor Daguerre is in here, I know he is. He's going around the ring one last time, but he'll leave again. He's angry because he thinks I talked Marthe into putting the books away. Even though I had nothing to do with it. I only gave her a hand. Or maybe the old bookseller thinks I'm going to move in. Maybe he thinks I'm going to put down roots here. But he's wrong. There's something else I have to do.

Chapter 9
The Garbage Dump

In fifteen years, Number Nine Park had hardly changed at all. The trees were scrawny, the grass was still yellowish green and the remains of another era were coming up to the surface like so much trash that you can't quite manage to forget. Years of burying garbage had turned this place into loose soil with constantly changing shapes, and no one was surprised to see mounds suddenly appearing in the middle of the baseball diamond or the parking lot. You would sometimes find rusty bolts running in neutral under the bark of a tree, and rumour had it that a grenade still licensed to kill had been unearthed near the fountains. Panic-stricken parents wanted the place shut down, but their children were against it because they had fun in this park. When Hugo got out of a taxi in front of the Motel Émard, two women came up and spoke to him at once.

"Even if you don't live in the neighbourhood it doesn't matter. We're asking everybody to sign. We need lots of names!"

"Sorry. I don't have time ... the taxi's waiting. I'm

leaving again right away."

"But this is about our children. They're liable to be poisoned if they play here!"

There was a vibrato in the woman's voice. Her name was Madame Blanche. She was a schoolteacher and in her spare time she dealt with catastrophes. In fact, that was why she was pointing to the park as if it were the anteroom of hell. It was a convincing act. Convincing enough, in any case, that Hugo gave in. He took the pen from her and scrawled his name on the sheet of paper.

And yet he was quite fond of this park. He had memories buried here. But he'd given in because it was politically correct to oppose garbage dumps.

"We're planning a demonstration, too. A big rally in the park on Sunday."

"For the solstice," added the other woman, the more timid of the two. "The summer solstice is on Sunday."

A real recorded announcement. They bombarded Hugo with their little ad campaign while following behind him, as if they wanted a commitment from him. A promise that he'd come.

"There'll be musicians and fire-eaters — and clowns."

He had long since stopped listening when he rushed into the flat-roofed little building that served as the motel's reception area. No messages for him, no mail or phone calls. He went straight to his room, where he collected his belongings at breakneck speed: the clothes he'd bought the previous week and hadn't tried on yet, the brand-new suitcase and the book with silky pages he still intended to read. For once, Marthe was free this weekend. She had invited him to spend a few days with her, to give him a break from this gloomy room, and he'd agreed without hesitation. As he was closing the door he ran into Madame Blanche and her associate and waved to

them. Stepping into the taxi, he told the driver:
"Éliane Street!"

Marthe had not really quit her job at the library. She'd just taken unpaid leave — for now. The decision had nothing to do with the arrival of her half-brother, she maintained. She had been thinking about it for a while. But the least you could say was that everything in her life was on the move. First the massive tidying up of the books, then her rehearsals with the Lexiphone, which were more and more frequent, and finally this rather wacky invitation: a weekend on the couch in front of a TV set with no picture. What better way to get a change of scene! The money from Barnum's still hadn't arrived, the rent for the Motel Émard was starting to dig a hole in his budget, and four days on the house at his half-sister's place wouldn't hurt. Especially since they were getting along so well.

At first he paced the living-room, orbiting the sofa and the blue glow. To put on a brave face he pretended he was reading Baudelaire, but he relinquished the book very quickly because Marthe was asking him all kinds of questions. She wanted to know what the circus was like. Whether the lion-tamers ever got scratched, whether the acrobats ever fell, how the knife-thrower managed not to injure anybody. Sally's ghost came and prowled for a moment, Hugo began to stutter and Marthe fell silent.

To get some fresh air that evening, they crossed the little square in front of the house and walked slowly up Delorme Boulevard. They talked about this and that, about the rumbling discontent in the neighbourhood because of the roadwork that would be starting one day soon. Like Hugo, Marthe was of two minds about cleaning up the park. If everything was destroyed, she would be leaving some memories there.

Without discussing it, they walked past the Motel Émard, crossed the big parking lot, then dived into the park. It was Marthe who pointed to the bench in front of the big battered field. Hugo nodded and they sat down. They must have been thinking about the same thing, about the encounters they used to have with Victor Daguerre, about the picnics where they used to tear each other apart. But neither of them felt like talking about that. They preferred to breathe the fresh air.

Hugo enjoyed the easy relationship between them. Marthe had her apartment, she played music whenever it suited her, and when they both felt like it they'd do something together. They sat there for a good half-hour, reflecting silently. Then he asked point-blank:

"Remember the other day, when we went to the lake? What happened exactly?"

Marthe's reply had been ready for a while now and she rhymed it off like someone saying a prayer.

"I felt really sad for a minute when I went out on the veranda. That's all. It's over now."

He didn't believe a word, of course, and continued spying on her out of the corner of his eye. For a moment he thought she was going to get up, slip off, walk away. He pressed on.

"Gaël. Who was she yelling at when she went outside?"

Now her back was up against the wall. Her upper lip began to quiver and she whispered reluctantly:

"At him. She was running after him."

Hugo wanted to laugh. He himself had gone running through the big house after Victor Daguerre the first night he'd slept there.

She was at one end of the bench, about to fall, ready to topple into the garbage dump, and the words still wouldn't come. She was trembling, her fingers were running over the bench, and then she came out with it in one go.

"At the cottage, Papa and I made love. I was seventeen and it's as if it happened yesterday."

Hugo shrank back. There'd been a misunderstanding, they weren't talking about the same thing. When he asked his question, he'd been thinking about that night when they'd smoked the grass.

"Mama didn't want to go to the country any more. She was too sick and she preferred to stay home ... near her doctor."

This time he was the one who wanted to get up, to move away from the bench. Her words had shocked him. He clenched his jaw and didn't want to hear any more.

"Papa and I were at the cottage. The first night, he came to my room. We talked about Mama, about her sickness. He was affectionate, but there was something different. I don't know how to say it. He touched me, something he'd never done before. We were both crying because we knew she was going to die. It might take a long time, but eventually the Parkinson's disease would kill her. I was inconsolable and he lay down beside me, the way he used to do when I was little. He had the same odour — it was reassuring. It seemed to me that if we stayed there, clinging to one another, the pain would go away."

"What are you saying? What's this all about?"

Hugo was terrified, but Marthe couldn't see that. She went on in the same monotone, determined to get to the very end.

"I didn't feel anything. He was consoling me, that's all I remember. Mama was going to die, I was terribly sad. Then I noticed that there was blood on the sheet. There was blood and I realized that it was done, it was finished. In my mind it couldn't be bad. He'd done it because I was afraid."

Marthe was looking straight ahead, imperturbable. Only her upper lip betrayed her emotion.

"The next day we talked. We got drunk on words. We were stunned, imagining that nothing had happened — or that it was perfectly normal. The doctor had just told us something unthinkable. At times like that, you give vent to your grief however you can."

Hugo was sorry he'd asked the question. The gulf that was opening before him was throwing him into a panic and he wished he could go away. He wanted this conversation to end, wanted this horror story to be choked off, to go hang itself. He wanted to go back to the sofa and sleep, just for a while. To escape this nightmare and dream about the circus, perhaps.

"We stayed at the cottage for five days," Marthe went on. "And on every one of those days, we started again!"

"Stop! I don't want to know! Be quiet!"

"Later on, he wasn't the one coming to my bedroom. I was going to his. I couldn't stand being alone. I wanted to be with him. I wanted to disappear under him."

"Marthe! Enough! I'm going!"

He got up, but she kept him there a while longer. She pulled at his sleeve until he turned his head, until he was looking deep into her eyes.

"And do you know what he told me after those five days? Do you know what he finally told me?"

Hugo didn't want to hear that either. He would rather have talked about the knife-thrower and the trapeze. About Sally's death, even, which all at once seemed to him less painful.

"He told me that I wasn't his daughter. That my

mother was already pregnant when he came into her life."

"That's not true! What are you talking about? That's crazy!"

"That was what I thought too."

"He was feeling guilty! He'd have said whatever came into his head!"

Hugo's anger made Marthe pull away. He was beside himself and for a moment she thought he was going to do something stupid.

"That son-of-a-bitch! Screws his daughter and then, to make everything neat and tidy, he decides that he's not her father, that she's somebody else's. That's disgusting!"

"Except it's true, Hugo. As true as you and me sitting here on this bench."

He still wouldn't believe her, shaking his head and pounding the bench with his fist.

"You can believe me, Hugo, I swear. My mother got pregnant accidentally, by a man she barely knew and wasn't in love with. It wasn't till afterwards that she met your father. He was moved by her situation, I think ... and that was how he came into her life!"

Marthe was biting her lip. At the other end of the bench, Hugo unclenched his fists and stuffed his hands in his pockets. The park and the garbage dump were a rose garden compared with what she'd just told him. Fortunately she said nothing more. She just looked at him.

They stayed there in front of the battered field for another good half-hour. Then, when they got up, she offered him her arm. Hugo had a broken wing and he was limping as if he'd run the marathon. She was tired too, and her voice was nearly gone. They went home in silence, separated at the foot of the stairs, and Hugo didn't even bother to turn on the TV. He undressed in the dark, she played a few arpeggios upstairs and he fell asleep before she'd played even one entire piece.

Chapter 10
Marthe

I can understand why Hugo is feeling unnerved. For years I used to think Victor Daguerre was lying. We'd had that odd relationship, that great "festival of consolation," and then to ward off bad luck, to erase the unacceptable, he had told me that I wasn't his daughter, I was someone else's. For a long time I carried that doubt, that burden, and I understand why Hugo is putting up resistance. He refuses to be someone else, because that would force him to untie the knots, to go back over lots of things in his own life and start again. He hasn't chosen to do that yet. It's his right, but I don't want him to leave, I'd like him to stay. I know it's hard for him. I'm not his half-sister any more. I'm not anything at all.

When I woke up there was a cool breeze. June won't be quite so blistering hot today and maybe we'll be able to talk. There's a part of me that's obsessive. There are a few things I need to clarify. About my mother, for instance. She was the one who was supposed to die first, and the reason Victor Daguerre took me in his arms was to console me. But he went before her. He collapsed in the back of his bookstore, heavy as a tombstone.

She was the one who was supposed to be taking her bow, but she stayed. She lingered on for a little while to tidy things up. Even though she was dying, she wrote a new role for me and gave it to me one morning. It was like getting news from some distant world. The writing was crabbed, illegible in places. Yet it was all there in black and white. Nothing I'd believed till then was true.

I carried that letter around for years. I reread it a hundred times, a thousand times, I kept it in a box with my jewellery, my souvenirs.... I've learned my life by heart, so to speak. I kept it near me like a musical score, till it was inscribed in my memory, till I knew all the notes. And then one day I put it away with all the rest.

Now I want to find that letter again. Even if I have to open all the boxes, even if I have to take all the books back out, I want to get my hands on it before he finds out about the rest, before we come to talk about Charlie. I like Hugo. Often I feel like taking him in my arms and rocking him. But I hold back. I'm afraid he might run away.

Chapter 11
The Parade

Marthe spent an agitated night. She was torn between the thought of going back to it — talking with Hugo until he knew everything — and the desire to drop it. The desire to feel comfortable with him and not dig up anything else.

The phone got her out of bed. More specifically, Madame Blanche, the schoolteacher, who was also on the committee for closing the park.... The same woman Hugo had encountered outside the motel. The demonstration her committee was organizing would be a great success, but the entertainment side was not yet finalized. Marthe's good ideas were known in the neighbourhood and, as she was no longer at the library, perhaps she'd have some time to think about it.

"Give me a day," she said. "I'll call you back a little later if I come up with anything."

Hugo was fast asleep on the sofa. Buried in the cushions, he didn't even stir when she leaned across him. Still in her bathrobe, she went out to the garden to bring in the newspaper. The more she thought about it, the more amusing it seemed. She would prepare a picnic, as she'd done for their trip to the lake, and they would spend the day with the people from the neighbourhood. It would be another trip. Less ambitious than the last one, maybe, but still a change of scene.

Hugo got up much later, spent a long time in the bathroom and didn't finally come back on duty until just before noon. It was getting late, Marthe had promised to call Madame Blanche, and she was dying to know more about the demonstration. He groped around in search of coffee, she poured him a cup, and he gave her a little bow. From all appearances Hugo had had a bad night, but he was making an effort to hide it.

"I got a call this morning. They're looking for performers for the demonstration."

He said nothing.

"It should be fun. The whole neighbourhood will be there."

"But I haven't got a thing. No costumes, no makeup. I've lost everything."

"You could play the Lexiphone!"

"No, no! Anyway, you play a lot better than I do."

"But you're the performer!"

He stuck his nose in his cup and was very careful not to say anything more. Never mind, she spent the rest of the afternoon teasing him and pulling his leg. It was affectionate. She didn't want to force him, but it was such a fine opportunity.

Not a word, though, about what she'd said in the park the day before: not the slightest allusion, as if it had never happened. The weather was still hot, the humidity was unbearable and Marthe suggested they go down to the basement to cool off. She was not being completely disinterested. As soon as they set foot down there, she headed for a big closet, opened it and started rummaging through Victor Daguerre's clothes. The bookseller's black suitcoat would make a very fine dinner jacket. They'd just have to add a little colour, some sequins, maybe. A bit of face paint and the deed would be done.

Hugo was putting up less and less resistance. Just one little act in the neighbourhood park. Nothing to make a fuss about. Besides, it was fun to be fooling around with Marthe in these old clothes. They were like two children playing dress-up.

*

The following Sunday they were in the Motel Émard parking lot with the other performers from the neighbourhood. But Hugo was brooding. This was anarchy! There was no stage, no lighting, no PA system. How the show would unfold was a mystery but the organizers, headed by Madame Blanche, didn't seem worried in the least. They were handing out leaflets and selling badges at the entrance to the park. An ever-growing crowd was pushing and shoving through the stunted trees. Buses were lined up along Delorme Boulevard, and the nearby streets were disgorging entire families strolling along hand in hand.

Never had Marthe seen Hugo as nervous as he was now. He was pacing and asking himself how he could have agreed to do such a thing. At noon, the park was dark with people! The boulevard was blocked along its entire length and bystanders were climbing onto the embankment.

"Somebody has to do something or there's going to be a disaster!" Hugo warned.

But no one else was worried. Even Marthe thought things were perfectly normal. It was like this whenever there was a demonstration in this park.

"Just do the best you can," she said. "People are glad to be here. It's been a long winter and now finally there's good weather."

"But I thought it was a demonstration?"

"It is a demonstration. But it's a celebration too."

"Marthe! Do you realize they won't hear a thing, they won't see a thing? There are two thousand people here, at least."

In the motel parking lot, each person was concentrating on his own act, but the order in which they were to appear had not yet been determined. At Barnum's that was crucial. The "parade" was what set the tone for the show. The performers would file past in groups, in order of appearance, and only after this ritual could things get under way.

Hugo took the Lexiphone from its case, muttering something that only he could understand. Then he counted the performers in the parking lot. If he wanted to avoid disaster, he had to take action. As if the role were his responsibility, he drew up a plan, a *mise en scène*. He began gesticulating in front of everybody, pointing to some and shifting others. It was a convincing performance. The artists got into line the way he asked them, and no one questioned the clown's authority. While he was at it, he turned to Marthe and asked:

"Could you write out the words to a poem? You know, from the book with the silky pages?"

"Baudelaire?"

"Do you know any of them by heart?"

She nodded and, without even trying to understand, pulled a scrap of paper and a pen from her purse. Hugo was already walking away. Holding the Lexiphone at arm's length, he was directing traffic in the parking lot. Everyone seemed to understand and little by little the parade was taking shape.

Marthe watched him while she scribbled some verses on the back of an envelope. The more he moved around, the greater his self-confidence. Time was short, the sun was at its zenith and the demonstrators wouldn't wait much longer. She would have to move quickly.

She had chosen "Elevation." In her opinion it was the most suitable of the poems. She had played it several times in her apartment and the result had astonished her every time. When Hugo came by, she was given another bit of information: he was going to lead the parade. She would hold the poem in front of his eyes and he'd bellow the words into the Lexiphone, hoping that everyone would hear. As for the subtleties in the text, they'd have to come another time.

When the start of the parade became imminent, Hugo played a few scales to warm up. The musicians, magicians, fire-eaters and impersonators were behind him, and when he raised his arm for the starting signal they all moved as one.

The Lexiphone had neither the strength nor the intensity of the trumpets, trombones and drums. It was through mystery that it touched people's hearts: a sound, a murmur, a breath of wind that whistled, swelling constantly.

The crowd moved aside to let them pass. The "parade" then traced a heavy line through this opaque mass and the hubbub that had prevailed a few minutes earlier was smothered completely. Those who were farther away, along the embankment and on the boulevard, pricked up their ears, climbing onto one another the better to hear. Hugo played oddly, actually. He declaimed like someone shouting orders during a demonstration. The Lexiphone had become a megaphone and the words were absolutely appropriate.

"... and purify yourself
by drinking as if it were ambrosia
the fire that fills and fuels Emptiness."

While he played he was watching Marthe out of the corner of his eye. He was reading so forcefully that sweat was standing out on his forehead and drowning his eyes like tears. With the echo, it was like listening to four or five instruments: flutes, clarinets, violins. All along the parade route people were snapping pictures — and they were all fascinated by this music. In fact, Hugo was playing his soul. And his soul must have resembled many others, because people were listening to him in total silence.

When he came to the middle of the field, he turned right, initiating a major shift. The performers formed a semicircle and the stage appeared, carved out of the crowd. This was where Hugo's contribution was supposed to stop. According to the plan they'd drawn up, a violinist and his accompanist were supposed to take over now, followed by a juggler and an Elvis impersonator. He touched Marthe's arm lightly to let her know that it was over, that he was going to stop. She nodded, folding up the envelope. A man in his forties leaned towards her.

"Are you with the Jehovah's Witnesses?"

Marthe turned towards the insolent individual. He had a black moustache and wore his hair combed back. She crucified him with a look while the Lexiphone's final echoes died away. Hugo hadn't heard the remark, but he thought he recognized the accent. Turning his head, he found himself face to face with Bobby, the knife-thrower. His knees gave out, his head spun, and as he was falling his thoughts turned to the Lexiphone. He mustn't break it, it absolutely had to be saved. The music his half-sister — or was she? — drew from it was so beautiful, so unusual.

The spectators as well as the performers were puzzled by his manner of exit. He seemed to be losing consciousness, to be passing out. As agreed, the violinist started to play. All eyes turned immediately in his direction and no one showed any more interest in the clown who had led the parade.

Hugo recovered, but he was confused. The man who had frightened him so badly was bending over him and there was nothing threatening about him. In fact, aside from the moustache and the hair, he didn't look the least like Bobby.

Marthe had displayed a great deal of tact in this situation, which could have been embarrassing otherwise. With great dignity she picked up the Lexiphone, which was intact despite its fall, gave Hugo a handkerchief to wipe his face, took his arm and led him to the Motel Émard parking lot. Someone gave them a cognac and the organizers filed past to thank them. Not one word, not one remark about his exit. Instead, he was offered another drink before he'd finished the first.

The show was going full tilt. More people were arriving and the committee members were congratulating each other on their success. There was sure to be something about it in the papers tomorrow. Marthe had moved away to listen to the music. Someone had given Hugo a third glass and, to be polite, he had accepted. But he drank it very slowly.

Chapter 12
The Long Weekend

When Hugo woke up next morning, slumped among the cushions, he scowled. His left wrist hurt. He'd injured it when he fell. The cognac had helped numb the pain, but this morning his whole hand hurt. So did his head.

He thought about Bobby again. About the false Bobby who had given him such a scare. If he'd had that reaction, it meant that the real Bobby was still around somewhere, that he hadn't disappeared altogether. Heavy-eyed and short of breath, he looked around, asking himself a lot of questions. How had he got back to the house, for instance? He didn't remember a thing, except that at a certain point the supply of cognac had dried up.

He tried to get up, take a detour through the kitchen, see if there was any coffee, but changed his mind when he lost his balance over the low table. His gait was precarious to say the least, and he didn't push it, but fell back onto the sofa and dozed there for a while longer.

Marthe must have been awake for a while now. She was playing the Lexiphone upstairs. Half awake and half asleep, he wondered all the same what she might be saying into the instrument. Great works, most likely. The most beautiful texts she'd come across in her reading, probably. Marthe knew so many things.

His head was heavy and the slightest movement took considerable effort. He got up again. His gait was a little more confident. This time he got as far as the front hall before he had another dizzy spell. Clutching the door, he went out to the garden for some fresh air.

The music had stopped. He thought again about the previous day. About the way he had bellowed the poem into the Lexiphone. The difference between his own performance and what he had just heard was like day and night. Two different worlds.

He took the newspaper wedged between two bars of the gate. Normally he'd have ignored it, but this time he couldn't help leafing through the paper. There was a photo on the second page. He and Marthe were very conspicuous, along with all the performers who'd taken part in the celebration. The article talked mostly about the environmental dangers posed by the park, but under the snapshot there was a kind word for the former Barnum and Bailey clown, the unexpected visitor who had set the tone for the rally.

Slowly Hugo walked back to the house, wondering how they could have known about him. Who knew about his past? Unless he'd done some bragging himself after a few drinks too many. Still, he was not unhappy. The photo was flattering and the comments were quite complimentary. He had even felt that little shiver, the one he used to experience when he read reviews in the big newspapers. Sometimes they would talk about the knife-thrower, the clown and the pretty young woman who appeared with them.

He went back inside feeling more cheerful, but the

heat and humidity had turned his legs to rubber. Without pushing it, he took a detour in the direction of the sofa to stretch out his bones. Marthe couldn't be far away. When the music stopped upstairs, she never stayed there very long. But he didn't have the strength to lift his head and see.

"What do the papers have to say?"

The voice came from the staircase. The delivery was slow, still sleepy.

"I heard a report on the radio this morning. I bet you in three days there'll be a crane in the park. They'll dig, they'll take away everything they put into that hole twenty years ago...."

He ventured a glance and saw her sitting on the third step. There was something different about his gaze, about his behaviour too. She felt like laughing.

"Are you all right? How did you sleep?"

Nothing.

"Cognac's terrible stuff."

Hugo tried to play it down. Maybe it had been the heat or the humidity. He pretended he was asleep, muttering just a few words to avoid giving himself away.

Marthe descended the three steps and went to the sofa. As he was playing dead, she looked at the photo in the paper. She was about to sit down and read the article when there was a knock at the door. Hugo shuddered slightly. He didn't want to see anyone. His sofa was all topsy-turvy and he didn't look well.

"It's nothing — someone to pick up a book."

He frowned; she moved away, a little more awake now.

"I lend tons of books to people all over the neighbourhood. I've got things here they don't even have in the library."

Hugo pulled the blanket over his shoulders, then over his head. Never before had Marthe talked to him about this. But it was entirely possible. Yesterday in the park, he had seen that everybody knew her. He curled up in a ball and held his breath while she opened the door.

It was a man. A man's voice. An odd conversation, moreover. Marthe was all apologies, trying to hold back an outburst.

"You're right. My mistake. I'd completely forgotten...."

"But I told you. I even called the library to remind you."

"Look," said Marthe, "I'm taking a few days off. I left my datebook there. I just forgot."

"I'm sure ... but I'm working today. I don't get a long weekend."

"All right, okay. But it's going to be a little complicated. There's someone here."

"Look, Marthe, I don't care about your private life. I have to go to work. Bye now."

"I understand. Look, I'll figure something out."

"I'll be back around five."

Feeling ridiculous on his sofa, Hugo tried to extricate himself. Maybe he could roll himself up in the blanket, mummify himself so he could take a leap to the bathroom. He felt like a lover surprised by his mistress's husband. A scrap of anger turned his stomach and he stuck his head out to see what was going on. A child of eight or nine, a boy, was standing in front of the low table. He appeared to be at a loss, looking around as if he couldn't believe his eyes.

"Where're my books?"

Hugo was stunned. The child looked like Marthe, like his memory of her at that age. The same determination, the same obstinacy. He walked around the sofa and over to the main staircase.

"I want my books back. I built a city here. That's mean!"

Marthe was still talking to the man, who was trying to leave. Hugo stuck his hand out from under the covers and grabbed his clothes. He was about to pull on his pants when he stopped abruptly. What if this was Victor Daguerre's child? In a panic, he counted on his fingers. The boy was maybe ten years old. The business with Marthe and the bookseller went back to the early eighties. It was impossible. Relieved, he went on getting dressed.

The child was making such a racket! He was kicking at everything in his way. After he'd gone around the room, while he was still waiting for Marthe, he appeared in the living-room again and lit into Hugo.

"Was it you that took my books?"

"No, no ... I think they're put away upstairs. Who're you, what's your name?"

"Charlie. What's yours?"

Marthe stepped between them. The door was shut, the man had left and she was trying her best to stay calm.

"Charles, this is a friend of mine. His name is Hugo."

As explanations go, it was rather brief. What was between them went well beyond friendship. But Charlie couldn't care less. The disappearance of the books had him hopping mad. The books he'd used to make his cities had all disappeared. Philadelphia, which he'd erected in the dining-room, Chicago in the entrance to the living-room, and New York in the front hall.

"Why'd you tear them down?"

"Hold on now, I'll explain," said Marthe.

The child was already on the stairs. He was climbing the steps four at a time, shouting at the top of his lungs:

"It took me a lot of time to make Chicago!"

"Charlie, will you hold on a minute. I'm going to tell you what happened."

She set off after him and they disappeared at the top of the stairs amid a terrible racket. Hugo rubbed his eyes, asking himself if he was dreaming, if it was the aftermath of the cognac. He had noticed those strange constructions on his first visit. It had never crossed his mind to attribute these "works" to a child. A coincidence, that was all it was.

Marthe and Charlie had gone into the back bedroom, the one that was always closed. Hugo could feel anger rising inside him. He quickly grabbed his belongings and had just one thing in mind: to leave here as fast as he could. To get out, go back to the motel. For a while now they'd been walking on a tightrope, he and Marthe. They'd been working without a net. And she had never told him about Charlie. It wasn't that he hated children, far from it, but if she had neglected to tell him something that important, how could he believe anything else?

He hesitated briefly over the book with the silky pages. If he took it away he'd have to come back, return it ... and in his present state he was incapable of making such a decision. Leaving Baudelaire behind, Hugo went to the door and left without making a sound.

Chapter 13
Roadworks

The day after the demonstration, the perimeter of the park was sealed off. All the exits were closed, yellow tape was put up pretty well everywhere and on Tuesday a big crane was brought in. There was something melancholy about the sound of that machine. Like a breathless dinosaur digging its own grave. Three days later the crane had burrowed several metres into the ground. The operator's cab had disappeared completely and all that could be seen was the big arm walking its sorrow around the block.

I have a ringside seat. My room at the Motel Émard looks out on the work and I can follow its progress, understand its logic. They've thought of everything. Every day, a procession of trucks goes down into the entrails of the park to collect its alms. There was a terrible clutter of odds and ends hiding down there. Rejects, remnants and relics emerging every which way from that big gut. A little like a photo album: every page a different era, a different memory.

It's very entertaining. The park has never attracted so

much interest. Gawkers walk along the yellow tape, peering into the hole to see if they recognize anything down there. Evenings, in contrast, everything comes to a standstill. No one dares come close, maybe because they're afraid of falling into the garbage. That's when I enjoy going for a stroll. I walk along the precipice as if it were a high-wire.

I haven't spoken to Marthe since the weekend. She has left two messages at the desk. Actually, I'm worried. Maybe I over-reacted. She's entitled to whatever children she wants and she's under no obligation to tell me about them. In fact, I got carried away. It was the show the day before, maybe. Or the cognac. A nasty cocktail.

I should have phoned the next day, told her that I was sorry. Well, that I hadn't meant ... but I didn't dare. Since I've waited all week, it's even trickier now.

What bothers me about this whole business is the fact that Charlie was there from the beginning. His cities and the closed room at the end of the corridor. It seems to me she could have mentioned him.

I've been imagining all sorts of scenarios. That business with Victor Daguerre: what if she made it up? If she actually took it from a book? The episode at the chalet and the bookseller's confession. Maybe she invented it all. Maybe he really was her father.

I don't know what to think any more. I don't know what to do. And I'm still not returning Marthe's calls. I just stay here watching the big crane dig its hole and I wait. But I'm not the only one. Barnum's seem to be taking their time too. I phoned the bank in Florida yesterday. They haven't seen a shadow of a cheque pass through. But things are always slow in July, the clerk told me.

"Don't worry! And have a nice day!"

I know the bank's script by heart now. But it's not worth hassling them. Better to wait it out.

Chapter 14
The Dressing-Rooms

Hugo let Saturday and Sunday go by, thinking Charlie was probably with her.

But he called her first thing Monday morning. Marthe was still off work. He babbled something about Charlie and she admitted she owed him an explanation. And just like that, she invited him for lunch. He tried to get out of it, but she insisted. She would fix a salad, they'd drink some red wine and they could talk. Sort things out a little. He let her twist his arm, she showed her irritation and he gave in.

"All right, I'll be there around noon. You're right, we have to talk."

Hugo was expecting major explanations, an exhausting outburst that would take him from Charlie's birth to a detailed portrait of the father, by way of the intrigues that had led to the big disturbance. But it was nothing like that. Marthe had fixed a pleasant lunch. The shutters were closed, a few rays slanted onto the table and she offered him a glass of wine. It was a Cahors, a good one, and very soon the atmosphere warmed up.

"It's a week now that I've been looking for that letter," said Marthe.

"What letter?"

"I told you about it. My mother wrote me a letter before she died. You'd understand everything if you could read it. You'd see he wasn't my father."

Hugo wasn't interested in knowing anything about Victor Daguerre, or about this letter that would establish the so-called truth.

"Is that what you do all day long, rummage through those boxes?"

Marthe glared at him. He guffawed and she realized he was teasing her.

"I play music, too," she replied. "I practise every morning after breakfast."

Her eyes lit up when she talked about the Lexiphone. She couldn't help herself; the instrument and its music had cast a spell over her. She knew that Hugo's eventual departure would mean an end to her rehearsals. The final note of a piece she'd been working on for days now. In fact, that was one of the subjects she wanted to talk about. Yet they were eating in silence. The food was delicious. Hugo commented on the wine, which he thought was better than the one they'd drunk before, but there wasn't a word about what had brought them here. It was only with dessert that Marthe came clean.

"Since Jean-Philippe and I divorced, things haven't been easy between Charlie and me."

"Hold on a minute, I don't understand. What divorce? Who's Jean-Philippe?"

"I was married. Not very long. You know, everybody's been through a divorce."

He disagreed. He shook his head because it had never happened to him. But she was in no mood to argue. That was the way it was. It was hot, the weather was sultry, she had once been married and there was a storm in the air. The account couldn't have been briefer.

"Charlie stayed here with me after the divorce. And then one day, out of the blue, he asked if he could go live with his father. We'd quarrel like that now and then, but not so much that he'd go away."

"So he was the one who decided to leave?"

Marthe withdrew slightly. There was embarrassment in her movement, even shame.

"All right, I confess that at the end I tried to keep him. It became acrimonious. For a while I thought his father was up to something. That he was behind it all...."

There was a lengthy silence, an endless silence. The sound of cutlery on china only magnified their discomfort. Marthe nibbled at a piece of bread for a long time before saying:

"... so then Jean-Philippe remarried. Dominique, his wife, already had a child. Then they had a little girl together. It's a sort of family. And I think that's what attracted Charlie."

Marthe was speaking more and more slowly. Gradually she became lost in thought. She had only one son and he had deserted her. His departure had left a big gap.

"We see each other Saturday and Sunday, three weekends out of four. That's our arrangement. It's what he asked for."

He observed a slight trembling, in her fingers particularly. The cutlery was falling from her hands and her gaze was evasive. She got up, half numb, and asked if he wanted coffee.

Marthe was wearing a tight-fitting dress and her makeup was more noticeable than usual. She had prepared herself to entertain him. It was too bad to sink into gloom like this. He poured some wine, sipped it, then resumed:

"I'd like to see him again. We didn't talk much the other day but...."

"He never does. At that age they grunt. His pals are the same."

"Funny, I was thinking about him this week. What he said about his cities, the piles of books. It's weird, you know."

She came back to the dining-room carrying a tray with a coffee-pot and cups. She seemed a little more cheerful.

"There's something I have to show you."

She took some big photos from the nearby buffet and spread them in front of Hugo. They were bird's-eye views. Of big American cities. Especially those areas where the buildings were numerous and pressed tightly together.

"This isn't the first time I've had to tidy up. Last winter he built Los Angeles for me, right there in front of the door. It was terrible! You couldn't get through!"

She feigned anger but, truth be told, she found it amusing. She loved that child more than anything, and his absence was the tragedy of her life.

For a week now, in his motel room, Hugo had been telling himself that Marthe had lied to him, that he shouldn't believe her any more. But when she talked about Charlie any doubts he had were laid to rest. You can misjudge a sister, a half-sister and a false half-sister, but a mother can't be invented, you can't fake that.

They spent a while over the photos of cities — all of which Hugo had actually visited. She also talked about Jean-Philippe, about his job in an advertising agency and his marriage to Dominique. It had turned blazing hot.

Marthe was no longer finishing her sentences and the conversation was riddled with silences and sighs. Suddenly she realized that it was two o'clock. She absolutely had to rehearse; there was no question of putting it off.

"Stay a while. You can go back to the motel later, when it's not so hot."

"You're going to rehearse in this heat?"

"I certainly am!"

He bowed before such determination and immediately cast his eye in the direction of the sofa. He could stretch out there and, with any luck, he'd be able to hear Marthe's music.

He immediately spied the Baudelaire on the low table.

Marthe was in the bathroom and he stretched out his hand for the book. His eyes were heavy and he began stroking the silky pages, his head resting on the cushions. He liked this living-room, liked the way it smelled. A perfect place for a nap.

When Marthe emerged from the bathroom, drying her hands on her dress, all she could see were his feet resting on the arm of the big sofa. He wasn't stirring, he wasn't moving, and she climbed the stairs without making a sound.

*

She had been playing for at least an hour. Even longer, maybe. He'd had time to sleep, wake up and go back to sleep again. The thread of music escaping from under her door was an incantation. He was still holding the book. His fingers slipped between the pages and suddenly he had an urge to climb the stairs, to get closer and listen to the music.

First he went to the foot of the stairs. She was still playing. The melody was uncertain, even mysterious. A cry ... an invitation. He went up a few steps, but stopped right away. Maybe this wasn't the moment. She wanted to be alone, to concentrate on her music. For a quarter of a second he hesitated, then he climbed the remaining stairs, without thinking. She stopped playing right away.

"No, no, go on," he said as he walked in.

She was sitting on the bed surrounded by texts, poems, sentence fragments. Holding the Lexiphone, she might have been rocking her child.

"Please, play some more. I'd like to hear you."

He was fidgeting near the door; she was uncomfortable and began gathering up her things without looking at him.

"I was finished anyway. I've been here for a while already."

"Go on. Just one piece."

Marthe showed her irritation, got off the bed and went to the chest of drawers. She returned the Lexiphone to its case and looked out the window. She didn't seem well — her movements were jerky and she had to search for words.

"You don't believe me any more, do you? You think I'm making it up, you think I told you all that...."

"You know...."

"You won't admit it, I know that perfectly well. But something like that always shows."

He gritted his teeth. It was the music that had

brought him up here. And now she was starting all over
again. A fine rain was falling outside. The wind was
blowing harder and the curtain began to dance before his
eyes. The city was heaving a sigh after the terrible heat,
and in the street the blinds were opening one after
another. She leaned out the window and lifted her face to
the sky. The harder the rain fell, the more the city
bustled.

Like her, he moved closer to the breeze. This storm
had arrived just in time. He was prepared to believe
anything at all, as long as they stopped talking about it.
Down below, in the lane, two women were embracing in
the rain ... and farther away, two men were holding
hands. All the secret loves, all the tormented passions, all
the hidden affections were showing themselves in the
midst of the storm. These people, who normally kept to
the shadows during the daytime, were now racing
through the streets while the sky was unleashed.

Marthe threw her head back. This procession, this
parade, delighted her. So she wasn't the only one who'd
felt shaky. Joyfully, she flung her arm around Hugo's
neck.

"Look at them! I'm sure it's taken them a while to get
there. Because it does take time, you know, getting used
to what you are."

The storm was getting more and more violent. In the
square in front of the house there was a downpour. The
big trees were waking with a start, people were emerging
on all sides, half the city was outdoors and they were all
equally strange. Lightning slashed the sky and came to
ground in a street nearby. Farther away, others who were
seriously wounded, others who felt flayed alive, howled at
their windows. Hearts poured out into the street, water
overflowed the gutters, reviving forgotten odours, and

everything was carried away by the sluicing water.

A horrible uproar reigned over the city, and when the thunder pealed for the second time Marthe cried out. The noise shattered on the wall across the street, then came back to her like a punch. Leaning out the window, her face streaming, she yelled again, even louder. Her howls mingled with the sounds of the storm and spread through the whole neighbourhood. She was enjoying it, going so far as to make variations with her voice.

Hugo leaned outside too and for an hour they had a wild time. The rain was coming in everywhere, Marthe's big bed was inundated and, breathless, they stretched out on the floor. The final rumbling of the storm was lost in the distance. Farther away, near the door, it was dry. They crawled over and she came and snuggled against him.

As Hugo got his breath back, he grew tense. A sunbeam had just broken through. Its reflection danced across the wet floor and it was hard for him to let go. It was one thing to cry out to a ghost in the lane during a storm. But Marthe was clinging to his flanks. Her eyes were closed and she was smiling. Sighing feverishly, she kissed his neck.

Hugo was looking up at the ceiling. His pants were soaked, he was uncomfortable, he was looking at the ceiling, but now he didn't dare move.

Chapter 15
Hugo's Mother

When I woke up he had gone. It was dusk. Outside, everything was dry, so much so that I wondered if there really had been a storm, if Hugo and I really had yelled in the lane like lunatics.

The Lexiphone was still there in its case on the chest of drawers. We must have talked about it. I'm sure we'll come back to it. The light in the house is fluctuating between purple and gold. The sun is about to set on the little square and here I am strolling around naked. I don't know why, but for a while now I've been thinking about Hugo's mother. He never talks about her. Not one word since he's been here. Yet his mother was a fine person. She took care of him as well as she could. She did a lot, but then we always dream about what we haven't got. Hugo wanted to live with his father. Like Charlie.

A few months ago I'd have been incapable of walking around the house naked. I wouldn't have allowed myself to do it. It was the same with Jean-Philippe. Now I'm totally naked and I'm thinking about Hugo's mother. She never had any luck. She killed herself raising her son but he couldn't know that. She died when he was twenty. The neighbourhood is dead too. There's nothing left.

I'm thinking about her to defend myself. Because it's my story too. I didn't tell him everything at the outset. But Hugo is probably hiding things as well. I'm sure that if you were to push him in the right spot he'd admit to missing his mother too. He'd remember why we don't always say everything there is to say.

I love Charlie. But things don't always go the way we'd like. He doesn't know how to read. He should. At school they knock themselves out trying to teach him. Whenever he sees a book, it makes him think of a city. At first that was sweet, but you get tired of it in time.

I don't know where he gets it from, but there's a delinquent side to Charlie. I wonder what Hugo's mother would have done. As for me, I've sometimes gone a little crazy. One day I kicked his behind. Just thinking about it makes me sick to my stomach.

Night is falling. It's going to turn cooler. I've taken out a carton that escaped me till now. A box filled with family souvenirs. Maybe that letter is inside. I haven't lost hope altogether, I always find my way through my own disorder.

When I walked past the living-room I noticed a paper bag on the low table — and the Baudelaire too. That's strange, I thought Hugo had taken it with him.

Chapter 16
The List

He didn't get in touch with her again until the following Wednesday. Immediately Marthe invited him over and they had lunch together: salad, of course, and fruit like the last time, but instead of Cahors they drank tea.

Marthe was in a good mood. They talked about the park, about the edges of the cliff, which were stratified: superimposed layers two metres high. Where the big crane had cut a clear line, you could see the years shading off into one another. The discards from 1966, those from '65, from '64 — the year she was born.

But they were talking about the big hole to avoid talking about something else. Hearing praise of the garbage dump always bored Marthe in the end, and Charlie began skulking in her mind and wrinkles appeared on her forehead. She was imagining the worst. If a child had gone away like that it meant she was truly hopeless as a mother. She didn't pour out her heart on the subject, she kept it to herself, but it was a heavy burden.

It was hot. Hugo wasn't finishing his sentences and Marthe's head was nodding. Soon it would be one o'clock, she could go upstairs to rehearse, and he would lie down on the sofa. He would nap, and after that he'd go back to the Motel Émard.

"Tell me, is Charlie coming this Saturday?"

She did not reply right away. Out of caution, perhaps, or because it took her a while to come back to earth. Yes, Hugo was asking about the child. With her face half hidden by her teacup, she nodded.

"Am I invited? I'd like to see him again."

"That's all I do, invite you. I told you, my door is always open."

Pause.

"Not just that, Hugo, I think it's ridiculous for you to be staying in that motel. There's so much room here."

"I'm very comfortable there. For the time being it suits me fine."

Marthe merely smiled. She was happy about this date for next Saturday. She wiped her mouth, shook her head to get rid of the fog inside and got to her feet energetically.

"I'll clean up later."

That was the way she was, Marthe. Absolutely predictable. Hugo picked up his plate, she protested, he ignored her and she disappeared upstairs. Between the boxes of books and the Lexiphone, she hesitated. The letter that continued to elude her would simplify things so much. But she opted for her apartment and shut the door behind her.

Downstairs, Hugo poured himself more tea and munched some cookies. He was used to doing dishes. Sally had never touched them. After he'd put things away he went to the living-room, where he realized that the books were getting more and more numerous. Charlie had started a city on the other side of the sofa, and then there were the armfuls Marthe brought down every day. He wasn't unhappy to see them back. The sofa would be a little less lonely, the big room a little less naked.

It was as hot as ever, Marthe's music was more and more discreet, and Hugo picked up the Baudelaire as if it were an old habit of his. He slipped his fingers between the silky pages and began to stroke them.

Marthe had already stopped playing. The door to her apartment had just opened and there were footsteps in the hallway. As he couldn't get to sleep without that music, Hugo sat up on the sofa and opened the book. The pages glided beneath his fingers and he came to the lines he had recited in the park:

"Above the ponds and valleys,
above the mountains and woods,
the clouds and the seas...."

This was very different from what he had shouted. It was much rounder. Much warmer, too. He turned the page and read another poem.

There was a lot of noise upstairs. Marthe was emptying more boxes, leafing through every book. She made little piles that eventually blocked the hallway and soon she would come downstairs with an armful. He heard her go past, but he couldn't tear himself away from Baudelaire.

For an hour he went on reading, effortlessly, as if he were idling in a park. He stopped here because the view was breathtaking, there because there were rare birds. He was caught up in these poems; he couldn't always understand them, but they made him see pictures. He was overcome by these words that followed one after the other, that made him shiver.

Marthe was making a gallant last stand. She was turning everything upside-down and stepping up her trips to the living-room. She was more and more exasperated by this exercise. She was rummaging everywhere and she was unbearable.

He sank deeper into the silky pages. He would have stayed there all day, in fact, if someone hadn't come and knocked at the door.

"Do you mind answering that?" asked Marthe from upstairs.

Her tone was dry and there was nothing he could do about it. Marthe was obviously irritated. Reluctantly, he set down the book and went to the door.

"Sorry. I didn't mean to disturb you. I stop in now and then to borrow books...."

It was Madame Blanche, who had organized the demonstration. Today she was playing timid. She spoke in hushed tones as she shifted her feet on the doorstep.

"I ... umm, I wanted to borrow *Les Fleurs du mal*. By Baudelaire. That poem you read in the park — I'd like to read it again."

Hugo turned towards the sofa, trying to conceal his disappointment. Just then, Marthe's voice rang out upstairs:

"If it's Madame Blanche, I'm on my way down!"

"I thought it was so beautiful," the other woman said.

Hugo backed up to the sofa, grabbed the book with the silky pages and executed a little caper in front of the low table. A bit of fancy footwork to hide what he was feeling.

"I'm on my way," said Marthe again.

"All right, okay, I found it...."

Madame Blanche was bouncing up and down on the doorstep. She picked up the Baudelaire and said hastily:

"It's just for a day or two. To refresh my memory. There's music in those words. I knew that, but I'd forgotten."

Instead of leaving, though, Madame Blanche lingered in the doorway. She was looking towards the staircase, smiling blissfully. When Marthe finally appeared, Hugo left the room, thinking they had things to tell each other. Discreetly he withdrew to the kitchen, but Marthe's voice caught up with him:

"Hugo! There's a list on the desk in the dining-room. Would you be an angel and put the title and author under Madame Blanche's name?"

He had to look around for a moment before he found the ledger. The two women were whispering in the doorway. They seemed to know each other well and the little woman kept saying:

"Not at all. Things will get moving ... trust me."

This did not concern him. He didn't want to listen and instead began looking through the ledger, at what Marthe had called her list. To his amazement, a good fifty titles were in circulation in the neighbourhood — and some loans went back six months. He turned the pages and was reading the names of the authors when Madame Blanche finally left.

He didn't know what they had said to one another, but Marthe seemed upset. She stood there in the front hall, looking hesitantly at the door.

"I'm going out to get some fresh air!"

"I'll be surprised if you find any!"

The last thing she felt like doing was laughing. She was irritated and she didn't care who knew it.

"Losing things infuriates me! It's negligence. Pure and simple negligence!"

"Look, Marthe. I couldn't care less about your letter. I'm prepared to believe you, to believe whatever you say, as long as we stop talking about it."

He joined this request with an irresistible grimace. Marthe had no choice but to agree and they stood for a long moment on the doorstep, teasing each other. He talked to her about Baudelaire, about the few poems he'd had time to read, and she asked him why he had let the book leave the house.

"I've got all the time in the world. There's no hurry."

Marthe found this touching. She was moved, and it wasn't until much later that she went out for her walk. She stroked his hand as she moved away and he watched her until she'd disappeared from sight at the other end of the square. She was heading for the park. As with everyone else in the neighbourhood, it had become a ritual for her to go and see where the hole was now.

*

The following Saturday, Hugo and Charlie arrived at almost the same time. Hugo would have liked to see Jean-Philippe, but the child's father had already left. Among his belongings was an aerial photo of Oakland. The city was easy to erect because it was very orderly and building heights were restricted because of the risk of earthquakes.

Marthe had prepared a snack. Charlie set to work right away and in just an hour one whole section of the California city was in place behind the sofa. Hugo handed him books, one by one, talking about the cities he had visited with the circus. New York, Philadelphia, Baton Rouge, Dallas, San Francisco. The boy was listening with one ear as he went on working. You never knew what he was thinking. He was so secretive, Charlie, so mysterious that you sometimes wondered if he was really there.

Marthe was not unhappy to see them playing together. She had entrenched herself in the dining-room and was watching them from a distance. The child was clearly less aggressive than usual. It was hell when he landed on Saturday morning and then wanted to leave an hour later.

Hugo enjoyed watching him work. He guessed at the moves he would make, he spoke on his behalf. Mimes always have the sympathy of the audience, who take pity on them. They put such dedication into their silence that in the end you carry them, you love them. And that was what Charlie was. A mime. A child very different from others, from those he'd known, those he'd met. Unpredictable, too. Miraculously, his power of speech returned:

"When you were in the circus, what did you do?"

Marthe, who had pricked up her ears, joined in right away:

"Yes, Hugo, tell him about the circus!"

The boy stopped working and dug in his heels in front of Hugo. His mother got up discreetly and came closer.

"Well ... ummm ... talk about the circus ... I'm not sure. I'd like to tell him about my act instead. The one I want to put on."

No reaction from Charlie. He waited, impassive.

"Right now, in my mind, I'm working on my comeback. A fantastic act ... with an elephant and music. The Lexiphone, of course, but played properly."

Marthe had stopped at the foot of the stairs. Never before had he talked to her about his plans. Hugo seemed more comfortable with her son than with her.

"It won't happen with a snap of my fingers, of course. It will take hard work and plenty of it. I'll have to find an elephant and someone to train it. We'll have to rehearse. Rehearse for a very long time. I want to make that elephant dance. I have very clear ideas about what I want. What movements. And of course it will have to be funny."

There was a touching moment when he talked about the crowd. Standing in the living-room, he bowed to the imaginary stands. And if you listened carefully you could hear the applause. Charlie's face had lit up. There was fire in his eyes.

"You mean you're going to buy an elephant!"

Hugo swept the room with his gaze, as if the remark had not been meant for him. Then, with a comical move, he pointed his finger at himself.

"Buy an elephant, me? I didn't say that. I said I wanted to put on an act. But to do that, I'll have to go back to California."

"Ah!" replied Charlie, seemingly indifferent.

End of the programme. He turned back to Oakland and admired his city for a moment. He still had things to do, and without wasting a moment he got down to work again. Marthe was thrilled. Hugo had kept Charlie's attention for a good half-hour with his description of his act. It was something she'd never been able to do.

Chapter 17
Charlie's Pain

I'm sitting in front of the air conditioner in the dining-room. It's a noisy old model but at least it keeps me cool. When I look left, into the living-room, I can see Oakland appearing above the sofa. The old TV set is losing ground. The big cabinet is covered with books and Charlie keeps going upstairs for more; there are books of every weight, every size, every thickness. Marthe doesn't like to say so, but I think it's getting on her nerves. She can't take the kid's casual way with books. It's not just that he doesn't read them, he turns them into piles.

Marthe's playing improves every day. She's rehearsing right now, upstairs. And in a while she'll be taking Charlie back to his father's. Things have improved since yesterday. I talked to him about the circus again to put him to sleep, then I talked to him about it over breakfast. And he asks for more. Marthe tells me that's very unusual. Usually he's not interested in anything. To the point that she's taken him to a psychologist. Without much result, as it happens. He doesn't read, he barely speaks and whenever he comes to Éliane Street he makes piles of books.

Marthe uses complicated words when she talks about him. Mild dysfunction, she mentioned. Sequelae of the divorce, apparently. In my opinion it's nothing at all. He needs a little attention, that's all. Okay, he's not exactly a chatterbox, but he can make himself understood. And sure, he doesn't quite fit the Daguerre mould, but he has a good head.

Charlie understood me when I explained that it's harder to put on a circus act here. Out on the west coast you can rent an elephant. You don't need to make such a commitment. You try it out for a few trials and if it doesn't work, you return it and try something else. He wants me to make some calls. He says there are elephants here too. It's quite funny. I promised I'd try.

They're about to leave now. Marthe is in a great mood. A fine weekend. Charlie hasn't completely finished Oakland, but I promised I'd help him next time.

"Next Saturday?"

"We'll see," I told him.

Marthe has come to give me a hug. Charlie's outside and for a fraction of a second I feel like holding her, pulling her to me. She is wearing her clinging dress, the one I like. I could feel her breath on my neck. She asks if I'll still be here when she comes home.

"I'm not sure ... I have to go back to the motel. I've got things to do tomorrow morning."

Chapter 18
The Second-hand Dealer

The next day, Marthe went over to the motel just before noon. Hugo hadn't come back yet, so she left him a note. Out of curiosity, she'd made a few calls. At first people had laughed at her. Nobody believed her when she said she was looking for an elephant. Then someone had given her a number. A certain McTavish whom she had finally reached. In all seriousness he had asked her:

"Do you want it stuffed or alive?"

In the thirty years he'd been in the business, McTavish had never let a client down. He promised her the animal in three days, and when Hugo showed up at the house she was still giggling.

"Do you realize what this means? You can order an elephant over the phone ... delivery included."

"We'll see about that. Some people will say anything. Anyway it's a little soon. I'm not ready. We'll have to find a place to house it ... and some money, too!"

She had thought he'd jump at the chance, throw himself at the animal like a wolf on its prey, but Hugo needed a lot of persuading.

"Let me think it over.... I have to work this out."

"What's the risk? Go on, phone the man!"

He was disconcerted by Marthe's enthusiasm. She hovered over him, asking questions. This haste was bothering him more and more. He still hadn't received the money from Barnum's, his resources were limited and he knew what was entailed in taking on an elephant as a boarder.

For an hour he paced the living-room, weighing the pros and cons, looking for a reason to refuse. But he couldn't come up with one, and in the end curiosity won the day. When he got McTavish on the phone though, he nearly hung up. The man was deaf. Not only that, he was a second-hand dealer. At lightning speed he launched into a staggering harangue. In five days he would have the animal — and at a price that would defy competition. Hugo would just have to pay a small deposit.

Hugo bristled. There was no question of paying out a cent before he laid eyes on the beast. But this McTavish wouldn't hear of it. Without the money, he wouldn't make a move.

The whole thing reeked of a rip-off. With the receiver plastered to his ear, though, Hugo couldn't bring himself to hang up.

"How much does he want?" asked Marthe.

"A thousand-dollar deposit. But I won't do it!" Hugo shouted. "Before I even get to look at it? That's way too much!"

He paced at the end of the phone cord. Marthe was nodding her head pointedly, but still he resisted.

"Look, let's talk again later. I have to think this over."

McTavish didn't understand. The words were making no impression on him and Hugo had to raise his voice.

"I SAID: I'LL CALL YOU BACK LATER! AFTER I

THINK IT OVER!"

Hugo disliked this second-hand dealer. He didn't inspire confidence. His deafness was too convenient, he could hear what he wanted to hear; and then there was the matter of the thousand dollars. Of course Hugo wanted to go back to the circus. Of course he was going to make a comeback. But he had to know what he was doing. He had to prepare himself, spend some time on it.

"Still, don't you think it's fun to buy an elephant over the phone?"

He wasn't sure he wanted to reply. In fact he wasn't sure what to think of this whole business. Never in his wildest dreams had it occurred to him to put on a show here. So he first had to get used to that possibility.

He looked for the book with the silky pages on the low table near the sofa, until he remembered that Madame Blanche hadn't brought it back yet. Too bad. He'd have liked to read it.

*

They were walking side by side on the pavement. They were walking in silence along Delorme Boulevard and night was slowly falling. Like other people in the neighbourhood, they were coming to check the progress of the works. Hugo was deep in thought. Marthe thought he was at the circus, rehearsing his act. Suddenly he asked:

"Basically, what bothers you about Charlie is the same thing Victor Daguerre used to criticize me for."

She nearly fell over. His words had caught her totally off guard and she began to stammer.

"I ... I don't criticize Charlie for anything! He's just completely turned in on himself, it's such a shame."

There were a lot of people on the outskirts of the park. Marthe was no longer sure of anything. This remark of Hugo's had upset her terribly. She tried to explain herself.

"Of course I'd be happy if he read now and then ... instead of building those piles of books all over the house. But I take him as he is! I don't see what parallel you're trying to draw between yourself and Charlie."

She would have debated the question for another hour. She'd have gone back to the flood if he had let her. But people were crowding around them. They wanted to see the big hole. This was no time to parade family problems. He put his arm around her neck and they barely looked in as they walked by. Marthe wanted to go home. Hugo was uncomfortable.

"Look, I just said it, like that. You're perfectly right. Charlie and I have nothing in common."

She was trembling, yet the weather was so hot, so close. She was feeling bad and he began to play the clown in front of her. Nothing special. A little caper, a hop over the yellow tape, two sideways steps ... to the edge of the cliff. It was all in the way he moved, and in his expression as well. He was good at it, that was obvious. Very funny, too.

A few people stopped. His performance had taken Marthe's breath away. Now he was pinching his nose and walking along the edge of the cliff as if it were a high-wire.

"Come back, Hugo, that's dangerous."

Clutching at an imaginary partner, he did a tango

step above the void. He appeared to be in control, but what he was doing was very dangerous. Marthe slipped under the yellow tape and held out her hand.

"Come on, we're going home."

When he saw the terror in her eyes, Hugo stopped at once. She was afraid for him. Afraid he'd fall into the hole. All for a laugh.

They slipped back under the tape. As they walked down the street, he put his arm around her waist. In the yellowish light of the boulevard they looked like all the others, all those couples who were out walking together.

"Know what we should do?" he asked. "Take Charlie up to the lake. I bet he's never been there."

Marthe shrugged. It was a long time till Saturday. For the moment, Hugo's arm around her waist was all she wanted.

"I thought about Germain too. He's trained horses all his life. I'm sure he'd enjoy looking after an elephant."

He was already at the circus. Everything was just a matter of production. Anything was possible.

"And Gaël, Germain's wife. She could teach Charlie beautiful words."

"What on earth are you talking about, Hugo?"

"Weren't you the one who said she talks like Baudelaire?"

"Well, I'm not so sure. I've heard things like that but — really, I don't see how she could help him."

There was a quaver in her voice. Marthe wanted so badly for Charlie to be able to read. She'd have done anything to make that happen.

They continued on their way and ended up at the little square, but still Hugo couldn't calm down. He was very excited about this second trip to the lake, and when they arrived at the gate she conceded:

"It's true, you know. I'm sure Charlie would love it! I'm not so sure Gaël can help him, but...."

Chapter 19
"Do you come from on high?"

The following Saturday they boarded the little white bus once again and for an hour they travelled through the dull, overcast day, along the grand boulevards and into deepest suburbia. Charlie was looking out in every direction at once and Hugo told him all sorts of things about the lake: about the giant horse-trainer, and his wife, who was almost as tall as him and who talked like a book.

Marthe was leaning against the Lexiphone's case. She was discreetly leaving them plenty of room while she took a mental inventory of what she'd brought in her basket of provisions. A veritable banquet: small dishes inside big ones, a white tablecloth — and enough food to last out a three-day siege.

Contrary to their previous visit, it wasn't raining today, and when the driver stopped at the road that led to the lake Marthe stepped cheerfully off the bus. In a wonderful mood, she led the way while Charlie and Hugo dawdled along behind. Though they hadn't announced their visit, Germain was waiting for them at the end of the road, dressed in his good suit.

"Gaël told me you'd be coming this morning. I took her at her word. She's almost always right."

How could she have known? How could she guess? Neither Marthe nor Hugo had said a word. There had been no phone calls, not even to Charlie's father. Marthe gave the giant a questioning look, and his only reply was a wink.

"And who's this young fellow?"

Charlie looked the giant up and down, unable to say a word. He was impressed, stunned even.

"Cat got your tongue? Forget how to talk?"

Hugo hurried to his rescue.

"This is Germain. He's the man I was telling you about."

And Marthe added:

"Germain, this is Charlie, my son."

"I didn't know you had a son!"

Hugo closed his eyes. When he was young he'd kept hearing that phrase. Now it reverberated in his head, dazing him. How many times had he heard people say to his father: "I didn't know you had a son!" He took Charlie's hand.

"Come on, I'll show you the lake! There's a lot of people in the summer, but it's still nice."

Germain was totally mystified. Marthe asked about Gaël, who had gone for a walk in the woods. While they talked they continued down the road. Charlie and Hugo were way ahead of them. When they turned onto the path to the chalet, the boy was already on the beach.

Marthe was thrilled to be there, but still she wondered how the giant's wife had known they were coming. There was an intriguing side to Gaël, Marthe agreed, but nothing of the mystic.

Once they were inside the little chalet, she chased

away all those questions and spread her banquet cloth. The house was as clean as before, but it was much too hot to build a fire. She offered Germain some iced tea. They exchanged a few words about the weather. Then Charlie and Hugo came rushing in.

They had come by way of the beach and now Charlie and Hugo were looking around the house. The boy raced all over, opening bedroom doors, going out onto the veranda, then coming back to the kitchen.

"Why didn't we come here before?"

Marthe dropped her work and bent over to him. Her reply was quite simple. It had never crossed her mind. Taking Charlie's hand, she led him a little farther away, in front of the window looking out on the lake. They settled into the sofa, and she described to him the summers she'd spent here, when the lakeshore was still deserted. When there was nobody here but the farmer and his son, Germain, the big little giant.

Hugo had taken over at the table. He took out the cheeses, the cold meat, the crusty bread and the Cahors. She had remembered to bring a corkscrew and he opened the bottle, inviting Germain to taste the wine. It wasn't long before he began to talk about the circus and the act he wanted to put on.

"For sure I'm interested," said the giant. "Horses, horseback rides, tourists — it gets boring, you know."

"I warn you, though, it's no picnic. I've found an elephant. At least I think I have. He'll have to be trained and that takes time."

"Doesn't matter. I'd like to have a go at it."

The banquet was expanding. Marthe had put an entire pantry in the basket. Hugo found caviar and truffles hidden under a little flask of cognac. He took everything out while he went on with his story: the elephant had to be taught to dance. To sublime music. Hugo himself would be the clown. At the risk of being flattened, he would go underneath the animal. Then he'd scramble onto its back, the way you climb a mountain. It would be graceful despite its enormous size — the music would make all the difference.

Germain wasn't sure he understood all the subtleties, but he was ready to give it a try, to plunge in head first. After all, Hugo had been with Barnum and Bailey. He must know what he was doing.

"You realize," said Germain, "an elephant's a promotion!"

With his powerful voice, the giant had just sealed the pact. Hugo rubbed his hands. He was listening to two conversations at once. Marthe and the boy were discussing something too. It was most surprising because he'd never seen them like that, embracing and clinging to one another. Maybe it was the trip, or the fresh air. They were sitting motionless in the old rocking-chair and only their lips were still moving.

Hugo lowered his voice. He was still talking about the project, but the urgency had gone. He enjoyed watching them from a distance. Charlie's head was resting on his mother's shoulder and his eyes were fluttering. There was a creaking sound in the doorway. Quietly, the door opened, and Gaël's first glance was for Germain.

She came up to the table, holding a bouquet of wildflowers. The giant stood up right away to kiss her and their joined silhouettes cast a shadow into the room. Gaël's hair stuck out in every direction, falling into her eyes, but when she spied Charlie she immediately pushed it back.

> "Do you come from on high or out of the abyss,
> O Beauty? Your gaze, infernal yet divine

indifferently showers favour and shame...."

It was Baudelaire! Marthe was right. The poet was hidden away inside this woman who, if you looked very closely, almost resembled him. Gaël waved the bouquet over Charlie's head, as if to drive away any evil spirits. She walked all around him, gazing at him with curiosity.

The boy's eyes were popping out of his head. This woman who hid a giant in her entrails moved very gently. She murmured words, inaudibly at first, then more and more clearly. It was very beautiful. Marthe recognized among others a passage from "Elevation." Then one from "An Earlier Life." When she recited "Evening Harmony," it was as if she were singing a lullaby.

Gaël improvised with breathtaking self-confidence. She seemed to know, to understand all of Baudelaire. But Charlie too! She knew that he was uncommunicative, that he didn't know twenty words, that he refused to read.

Did she have a crystal ball? Tell fortunes from cards? Surely that was why she chose the most luminous passages, the brightest verses from *Les Fleurs du mal*. Charlie's pain demanded the finest remedy.

Right under Marthe's eyes, she breathed the words into Charlie's thin little body, she decanted the most beautiful music, and the child walked into the language through the front door.

After all, it was to draw Charlie out of his secrecy that they had come up here. Sure, there was also the question of the circus, of Germain and Hugo working together, but this time they had really made the trip to heal the child.

Marthe was holding the boy's hand while Gaël declaimed. The most beautiful poems were unfolding in the little chalet and Charlie couldn't keep still. He resonated with the music and he kept asking:

"Why didn't anybody tell me about this before?"

*

The party in the chalet lasted till late at night. Marthe's banquet kept them awake until dawn, and more than once Charlie took the floor. He borrowed from Baudelaire, and when he spoke the lines he did so with Gaël's intonations.

Marthe couldn't ask for anything more. She nodded each time he opened his mouth, and if she didn't understand he grew impatient:

"I rule from the sky, a misunderstood sphinx...."

This party was like a hallucination, though Gaël had brought out neither grass nor pipe. It was all in the words. In the music of the words and in their beauty. Hugo was not familiar with these rhymes, he'd never heard them before, but he resonated with every one.

The boy continued to astonish them well into the night. Soon he got up from the table, his eyes heavy, and wandered through the room for a while, then stopped in front of the door.

"The sea is your mirror; you gaze at your soul...."

Was it melancholy? Or was sleep gradually overcoming him? Marthe got up, took him in her arms and opened the door to one of the bedrooms. She deposited him in a bed and quickly covered him.

Gaël and Hugo were putting the dishes away while Germain went out for some fresh air. Marthe hadn't come back. Probably she had dozed off beside the boy, and once everything was neat and tidy Gaël slipped away. Outside, the sun was about to come up; Hugo's legs no longer supported him, and he collapsed onto the bed in the back bedroom.

A few hours later, though, the squawking of vacationers woke him from a light sleep. It was seven a.m. A sunbeam slanted into the bedroom and, opening one eye, he spied Charlie bending over him.

"What are you doing? Can't you sleep?"

"Come with me. I want to see the lake."

"At this hour of the day?"

"Mama's asleep."

He took Hugo's hand and tugged until he got up. Like a sleepwalker Hugo crossed the kitchen and went out onto the veranda. The light was dazzling and there was mist on the lake. In the neighbouring cabins there was more and more activity. Charlie went down the steps and turned around to be sure Hugo was coming after him.

"Don't go too far. Be careful."

He approached the water, dipped one toe and stopped short. He was already shivering, but turning back was out of the question.

"Go on, go ahead! Jump in!" Hugo encouraged him.

First Charlie got his thighs wet, then his whole body. Behind him, Hugo flopped onto the sand. After splashing around for thirty seconds, Charlie got out of the water and started back towards the chalet, announcing:

"We have to come back here.... I really like this place."

Hugo was in a bad way. It would probably take him all day to recover from the night before. He turned onto his back, took a deep breath and murmured, sighing:

"That's what I said the first time I came here ... the

only time. I was around your age...."

"You mean you came here when you were little? Did you meet Mama?"

He bit his lip. If he opened the door, the boy would ask all kinds of questions. He'd have to explain everything, even the inexplicable. He'd never get out of it.

"Come here. I have to talk to you. There's something I want to tell you."

The air was chilly. Charlie was shivering and Hugo flung his arms wide open to take him in. He came and huddled against the man's legs and wiped his mouth on his trousers.

"Know what we're going to do when we're back home?"

The boy wasn't fooled. He could see what Hugo was up to, the evasion he was preparing so he wouldn't have to answer.

"... as soon as we're back at the house I'm going to call that guy. I'm going to buy his elephant. And Germain's going to look after it. We're going to work together."

It was magic. He just had to mention the circus and Charlie fell, letting himself be carried away completely. For a while they rocked together on the beach. The child was digging his fingernails into the man's back and the man was half asleep. The sun grew hotter and hotter and the child felt better and better in his arms.

"I want to paint a picture of your beauty...."

It was a compliment. Hugo had never heard it, but he nodded and hugged the boy even more tightly.

"But you never answered. How did you meet Mama? Was it here at the chalet? When you were my age?"

Hugo grunted without really answering. Charlie had a mischievous look on his face. That was one question he hadn't borrowed from Baudelaire.

Chapter 20
The Trapeze

When they got back into town late the next day, Marthe insisted that Hugo sleep at the house. When they got off the bus they took a taxi. Charlie fooled around till the last moment, outside Jean-Philippe's house. Then, as he was getting out, he murmured:

"I curse the paltry pleasures of the night...."

Marthe wasn't sure what to think about this linguistic phenomenon. The child had never opened a book and here he was, invested with some of the most beautiful language in the world.

"Some things can't be explained," Hugo had reassured her. "You shouldn't even try...."

His words had little effect. Charlie was standing in front of the taxi, putting up a big fuss instead of going inside. He was supposed to stay with his father the next weekend; it was the fourth Saturday of the month. But he wanted to come back to his mother's house. In a week, Hugo might have found his elephant. That was something he didn't want to miss.

Marthe had to take him inside and talk with Jean-

Philippe for a moment. Hugo followed the exchange from inside the taxi. The switch in schedule seemed to be causing a problem. Nothing was simple.

Marthe reappeared five minutes later, the taxi resumed its course and they didn't exchange a single word till they were back at the house. That often happened when Marthe saw Jean-Philippe. A grating deep in the soul, followed by tremendous pain.

Hugo knew the route to the sofa. After he'd switched off all the lights, he turned on the blue glow and walked around the sofa, like an airplane describing a big circle before touching down. He was ready to roll in the cushions, but then he stopped himself. Upstairs, she was already playing. A piece of music that always had the same effect on him. An invitation to the voyage.

He took up his position at the foot of the stairs. The door was ajar, the melody was lovely. He climbed three steps, four, five. She was still playing. He stopped in the doorway and glanced inside the bedroom. He couldn't see anything.

What irresistible music! He was about to step inside, to rush forward, but he stopped short. In Marthe's bedroom the floor had given way. Even worse, the lightbulbs around her makeup table had been transformed into spotlights. The effect was startling. Five metres from him, hanging upside-down on a trapeze, Marthe was swinging.

Hugo stood on his little platform and tried to back up, but no way. There was no more staircase, no apartment, no books. He was inside a big top and it was time for the show to begin. After dreaming about this for so long, he wasn't going to back out now!

Marthe was dancing above the abyss. There was no net. No second chance. And she was floating, soaring in thin air as if she'd been doing it all her life.

"Come on! It's not dangerous!"

She held out her arms as she flew past him. Cautiously he leaned into the void. The deep black hole ... and the ring far below. There was really nothing left of the house at all.

"Come on! It's not dangerous!" said Marthe every time she went past.

She was having a fabulous time on her swing. It was totally incomprehensible. And then there were the red tights she was wearing — just like Sally's! A leotard traced her outline against the black background. Marthe was slim, and wonderfully agile.

"I'll hold your hand. You can hang onto me! It's easy, you'll see."

Hugo wanted to — but he let her go past once more. Suspicion. Maybe this woman wasn't Marthe. Maybe this acrobat was an illusion, a mirage trying to draw him into the void.

"Hugo Daguerre! Come on! You'll have to believe me one of these days!"

It was her, all right. What she was asking demanded an answer. The next time she went past, he clenched his fists and jumped in head first. His feet left the little platform and immediately he knew that she was there, that she wouldn't let him fall.

They made two or three passes, Hugo nodded and she set him down on the little platform. He wanted to get his breath back, and his strength, and assure himself that all this was real. But there was no need. Marthe gave him a big smile as she went past him, he fell into her eyes, and the next time around he dived back in.

It was magic. They were flying above the ring. Clinging to one another, they soared and never looked down. Marthe had been waiting for this moment since their very first meeting. She'd hidden it from herself, she'd lied to herself, but this time she couldn't resist.

They swayed together in the void, they eyed one another greedily, they devoured one another with their eyes. They were so lost in one another that they couldn't fall — except perhaps in love.

Chapter 21
Joint Custody

When I woke up I was sure he'd be gone, but there he was, with his head in the cushions, sleeping like a baby. I took a good long look at him. I like Hugo. He doesn't always understand what's going on, but he never passes judgement. I'd like to keep him here with me for a while. He touches me, he makes me feel good. He brings Charlie back to me.

When he got up I knew right away he wasn't going to stay. He talked about the motel, the bank and Barnum's, all at the same time. He barely took a sip of his coffee. And now I haven't seen him for three days. But I spoke to Jean-Philippe. Charlie will spend the weekend here after all. From Friday night till Monday morning. We even talked about his possibly coming back. Actually that would suit everyone, including Jean-Philippe's wife, Dominique. Three children are a handful.

Mustn't rush things, I know that. Mustn't count our chickens ... but I've never stopped waiting for Charlie.

*

That was Hugo on the phone. For three days now he's been in negotiations. That man, the second-hand dealer, is keeping him on tenterhooks. Apparently he's found an elephant. The delivery date hasn't been set yet, but he's already preparing the ground. He's found an empty hangar somewhere on the South Shore, in the suburbs.

It's quite weird, this business of the circus, here in Victor Daguerre's house. Charlie's in seventh heaven. Hugo is putting all his hopes into it, but he's a little tight for cash. Yesterday I offered him some money, but I could see he was offended. I explained that I was doing it for Charlie. He didn't answer.

Tomorrow we'll have lunch together, but I had a hard time persuading him. He claims this elephant business is taking up all his time. I suggested he come and work here, give out my phone number. He's hesitating. It's a last bit of shyness. Besides that, I have to pull the words out of his mouth! Which by the way is not the case with Charlie. I don't know what Gaël did to him, but he phones every day now. He fidgets at the other end of the line. They make me laugh, Charlie and Baudelaire. He's memorized two or three stanzas just like that, and he'll quote them at the drop of a hat. I told him we have the book here at the house, the complete poems. He really wants to see it. Actually Madame Blanche has it. Hugo mentioned it. She borrowed it a few days ago. She doesn't seem to be in any hurry to return it.

Chapter 22
A Runaway

When Madame Blanche appeared at the door the following day, both Marthe and Hugo threw themselves at the book. A lovers' rush. The teacher pretended to notice nothing. Marthe covered it all with a big smile and showed the other woman to the gate. They were talking about something that was "finally on course," and Hugo realized it was about Charlie and reading. Apparently Madame Blanche was his French teacher, and Charlie's recent progress seemed to be the result of some long hard work. Marthe congratulated the little woman, patting her on the shoulder. When she came back inside she was in a magnificent mood.

"You can read it first, Hugo. I've got all the time in the world."

"No, you take it. I'm very busy just now. You can lend it to me at night, before I go to sleep."

Marthe held back a smile. At night they were on the trapeze. The book with its silky pages might fall, it might disappear into the abyss. They laughed in the front hall for a moment, and in the end it was she who kept it.

Hugo went back to the living-room to make some calls.

She was looking for something between the silky pages. One particular poem. But what she was really doing was spying on him. She hung around his headquarters, hiding behind the book. On the table was his story in a nutshell. She cared about these scraps of paper, these quickly jotted phone numbers and notes. The name of the second-hand dealer, an idea for the act "in gestation" and his bankbook.

He was a true professional, was Hugo. When he worked, an iron curtain came down before his eyes. His concentration was awesome. And Marthe walked away. She had things to do. Since she had her nose in *Les Fleurs du mal,* she might as well take advantage of it to refresh her memory.

In addition to "Elevation," the poem she'd transcribed for Hugo in the park, which she played again every evening on the Lexiphone, she had been very familiar with Baudelaire at one time. Today, if she wanted to understand what Charlie was saying, she had no choice but to go back to the source.

She took a seat at one end of the dining-room table and opened the book in front of her. Her pleasure was obvious. Reading the book now would be nothing like the obstacle race of her attempt to understand what Victor Daguerre had meant in her life. On the contrary, this would be a warm-hearted gesture that would bring her closer to her son.

She read for a while. She felt fine, but all the same she wondered what Charlie could make of these poems. She was leafing through the book, going along well-known roads, when all at once Hugo started shouting. It was the second-hand dealer! He was on the phone and as usual he didn't understand. Something about money again. The man always wanted more. Marthe settled deeper into her chair and observed Hugo from a distance.

He'd spent the last days of the week at her place, glued to the phone, convincing somebody here, pressuring somebody there. There was a possibility that he'd give up his motel room. Day by day the act was taking shape, but it also took up a lot of room. Hugo was in a state of permanent jitters and Germain wasn't doing anything to help. Twice a day, he called to find out what was going on.

As for Marthe, her time was completely her own. Two or three times she had scribbled her letter of resignation to the library. Each time, it had been delivered to the waste basket. It was clumsily written, and neither the tone nor the form was satisfactory. She put it aside till later.

Marthe also spent a lot of time on the telephone. Between calls from the second-hand dealer or Germain, now there were those from Charlie too. He was talking more and more, he was genuinely enjoying it ... and sometimes he came out with dazzling stanzas. The blossoming of this child had been sudden, almost brutal. She was trying to understand. She wished she knew how Baudelaire, through that woman who was so physically unattractive, had come this far, as far as the wonderstruck gaze of her son.

There was a knock at the door. Hugo, who was between calls, jumped to his feet. The bookseller in him had just surfaced. He hurried across the living-room and went to see who was there. It was a child bringing back two books. Immediately they began bantering. The circus jitters had evaporated for the moment.

"What about you, do you read books?"

The child protested. Said he didn't have time, he had too many other things to do. Hugo teased him as he checked the two titles off the list. He closed the door and went back to the living-room, peering at the jumble of book titles and authors' names. Some were illegible, but mainly there were dozens of books that were overdue.

"Marthe, don't you think it's time we tidied up this list? We could get a new ledger too. And call the people who've kept their books too long."

"Your father would be proud of you."

He certainly didn't want to resemble Victor Daguerre. Just the sound of the man's name made him shudder. But he did enjoy working with books like this. The neighbourhood people who knocked at the door at any hour, the furtive conversations. He had got in the habit of reading the jacket blurbs. It didn't take as long as reading the books but it gave you an idea about them.

Marthe too was stroking the silky pages. She stopped at the poems Gaël had declaimed the other evening: "An Earlier Life," "Beauty." She spent half an hour with "Evening Harmony," humming it as she read. It was a lullaby.

Hugo pricked up his ears. He was leaning on the armrest of the sofa. He was no longer interested in the list, the phone numbers or the scraps of paper. He wanted to listen. Perhaps this was what she said into the Lexiphone. This piece that always had the same effect on him. He went towards the front hall, but she looked up at once.

"Is everything okay, Hugo? Is everything going the way you want?"

He had stopped, like a cat hesitating to pounce on its prey. Her eyes were wide open, she could see what was coming, but she spoke anyway.

"You know, about the money, I didn't tell you ... I had an inheritance from my mother. What was left from her family. Along with the house, it's a fair chunk. I could help out ... with the elephant. I know you aren't thrilled with the idea but...."

He wasn't listening. His eyes had filled with mist and only the image of Marthe was still clear in the middle. He held out his hand. She nodded and stood up, as if it was unnecessary to say anything more. They climbed the stairs in silence.

*

Marthe had tossed a blanket on the floor; he was lying on his back and she was snuggling up against him. She was gazing at the ceiling, telling herself again that she felt wonderful, that she had wings and she was in love, when there was a sound at the front door. She decided not to answer it and held her breath. But now someone was kicking the door.

"Charlie!"

She bit her lip, but Hugo had heard. He opened one eye as he ran his fingers through his hair.

"It's not Friday, is it?"

"Never mind, I'll deal with it."

The pounding continued, making an infernal racket. Marthe slipped on her bathrobe and raced down the stairs. All at once Hugo felt ridiculous. Lying in the middle of the floor, naked as a jaybird. He jumped into his pants, quickly did up the buttons and followed Marthe downstairs.

Charlie was on the ground floor, pacing. His mother

was following close behind him, trying to find out what had happened. It was obvious that he'd run away. During the summer holidays an old lady looked after him and his half-sisters, Adèle and Caroline. Taking advantage of her momentary inattention, he had got on the bus and come here.

"Don't you think Jean-Philippe will be worried?" asked Marthe. "You'll have to phone and tell him what you've done."

"I told him I wanted to come back here and live with you. I like it here, with Hugo and all his projects. I hate it at his place!"

"But right now, today, does he know you're here?"

He didn't answer.

"Then go and phone him. And if you don't, I will. You know perfectly well I don't want any trouble!"

Hugo slipped between the two of them and pointed to the silky-paged book on the table.

"Did you see that? All those beautiful sentences of Gaël's are inside."

"They are?"

With no hesitation, he picked up the book. Marthe thought Hugo's intervention was inappropriate, but the boy already had his fingers between the pages. Like others before him, he was attracted by the softness of the paper.

Playfully Hugo ran his fingers up and down Marthe's neck. Her hair was still damp, and when she turned around he winked. Charlie took the book to the living-room, where he settled into the cushions and, to his mother's astonishment, began to read.

This was more than she could have hoped for. He was here, he wanted to stay — and on top of it all, he could read!

Marthe rushed to the phone. Her conversation with

Jean-Philippe was straightforward and direct. To her amazement, he confessed that he wasn't surprised by the turn of events. For a while now Charlie had had just one thing in mind: to go back to his mother's house. Maybe they should respect that wish.

Marthe put her head in her hands. Her ex suddenly conciliatory, and Charlie reading Baudelaire on the sofa! He had relinquished Oakland, he'd stopped thinking about the circus and he kept asking:

"Did Gaël really write this?"

"Seems to me she did," said Hugo. "We'd have to ask Marthe, but it sounds like her style to me. It's the same words anyway."

Marthe laughed. She was trying to stop giggling. The boy was taking it all so seriously. He was literally devouring the book, while Hugo gathered up his scraps of paper and his phone numbers from the table. Under other circumstances she'd have corrected him. Providing publication dates, the most important titles and the secondary sources. Gaël had nothing to do with *Les Fleurs du mal*. But she forced herself not to say so. It wasn't necessary.

Chapter 23
Towing Included

When Charlie was there, Hugo slept on the sofa. And he was coming back more and more often. The boy no longer had any interest in building cities. He sometimes enquired about the circus, but what fascinated him now was Baudelaire. Marthe herself was of two minds. A precocious child herself, she hadn't become interested in the nineteenth-century poets until she was eleven or twelve. Charlie wasn't even ten.

"You know, there are lots of other interesting books too. Here's one by Alphonse Daudet. I'm sure you'd like it."

She was wasting her breath; Charlie liked *Les Fleurs du mal*. It was particularly distressing to Hugo, who hadn't touched the silky pages for days now. The boy was holding onto it with such determination that he doubted he'd ever get his hands on the book again. Not to be outdone, Marthe put in her claim for it too. It was unbearable.

And so one Saturday morning they were all three at the house. Summer was making its last stand and the oppressive heat was keeping them barricaded inside. Charlie was reading, Marthe was playing the Lexiphone and Hugo was reviewing his remaining options. He'd heard nothing more from the second-hand dealer, which didn't surprise him too much. He didn't trust the man. He was afraid of being ripped off. And then there was the question of the thousand dollars, which Marthe had advanced him and which McTavish had already pocketed.

He was under no obligation to put on this act. Nothing was forcing him to. In fact, what was going on between him and Marthe was far more important. When they went upstairs, when they were on the trapeze, it was prodigious, magical. On the days when Charlie went to his father's, they slept together and couldn't drag themselves out of bed the next day.

The circus at any price? Maybe not. He was enjoying his little librarian's job. He had bought a new ledger; he was recopying the titles of overdue books and even calling customers. Since he had left the motel, since he had settled in here, he'd made it his pastime.

The last Saturday of the month, then, they were all busy at their tasks. A lethargic nonchalance behind the closed shutters. And then the phone rang.

"Hello?"

There was a pregnant pause. Hugo held his breath and started drumming on the little table. Eyes darting everywhere, he cut in:

"What is it? Is he hurt?"

Charlie could only hear the crackling of the telephone, but he knew it was about the elephant. He put down his book and came closer.

"I SAID: WHAT IS IT? IS HE HURT?"

Upstairs, Marthe had stopped playing. The door to her apartment opened and she stuck her head out. The more he found out, the more agitated Hugo became.

"I'm not looking for a dromedary. What's all this about a bump?"

With McTavish you went from surprise to amazement. First, there was the towing. You don't transport an elephant just like that. Fortunately, it was included in the price. But there were papers to be signed. More complicated than expected, not to mention the food; for a small supplement, the second-hand dealer offered him enough for a month.

"A thousand dollars extra! When is this going to stop?"

The second-hand dealer couldn't hear his anger. He made him repeat it, he was as slippery as an eel, and the only way to come to an agreement with him was to say the same thing he did. They arranged to meet at noon, in the suburban hangar Hugo had rented.

"Are you sure you got that?" he shouted. "Noon, the industrial park on the South Shore!"

He was shouting so loud that Charlie plugged his ears. Hands on his temples, he turned towards his mother when she came and stood beside him.

"Like a ship that awakens
To the morning wind,
My dreamy soul casts off...."

As he hung up, Hugo wondered if he had really made himself understood. The South Shore, the industrial park ... he hadn't given the street name, but it was easy to find. Charlie was hopping up and down around him. Absorbed in thought, Hugo got his jacket from the front hall and opened the door.

"Wait a minute ... you're not leaving just like that?"

Marthe had caught him. The boy too. Standing on the veranda, they both tried to keep him from going.

"Wait, I want to come too. I want to see an elephant up close."

But it was out of the question. The curtain had just come down again over Hugo's eyes. This was work. Dangerous work, even. He wouldn't have time to look after a child.

"Next time...."

The boy mounted the barricades. Ever since their trip to the lake he too had been waiting for this day. Not a weekend had passed that they didn't talk about it, didn't make plans. And now he was being shut out.

"Oh, I just remembered! I have to call Germain!"

Hugo retraced his steps, trailed by Charlie, who was pestering him.

"You walk on corpses,
Beauty, undismayed...,"

he yelled.

Hugo had other things to do, other things to think about. It was essential that he talk with Germain. He dialled the number and met Charlie's stupefied gaze as he stood on the bottom step.

"*I rule from the sky, a misunderstood sphinx....*"

The ringing phone made an earsplitting noise, Germain still hadn't answered, and Charlie was furious. The child raced up the steps four at a time. Books went flying on all sides as he climbed. He stomped into his bedroom and slammed the door as hard as he could.

It was at this moment that Germain answered the phone. The conversation lasted only three seconds. Things were finally starting to move. They had a date at noon. There was a loud cry at the other end — and Hugo hung up. It was only a small step between an exit stage left and a detour by way of Charlie. A tiny little effort. He was on his way upstairs when Marthe came and put her arm around his waist.

"Don't worry, I'll handle it."

He stopped on the first step and turned around. They exchanged a knowing look, he would have kissed her, but she walked with him to the door.

"Go on, you'll be late!"

*

The industrial park on the South Shore was ugly and impossible to find. It had been built within the limits of the city, in a place civilization was expected to expand to by the year 2000, but something had gone wrong along the way. The city had not covered the expected distance and the warehouses stood there, useless, like rocks in a field.

The last bus had dropped him off two kilometres away. It had taken Hugo twenty minutes in the blazing sun to cover the distance. Under normal circumstances he would have been impatient. But he was thinking about Marthe, about Charlie, about what had been happening to him lately. During the summer he'd played all the parts. Father, brother, mother and clown. The ultimate act.

When he finally got there, Hugo almost fell flat on his face. The building was a big aluminum cube with no windows or charm and a single door in the middle. Far from Éliane Street, far from indiscreet gazes, he could put together his act in perfect peace and tranquillity ... but what a depressing place! He had to come here, to the end of the earth, to get back to the circus again!

Germain arrived late, of course. He'd got lost and had to take a long detour before he got back on the road. Hugo greeted him in the parking lot, already worried.

"The second-hand guy's got lost, for sure! He said noon. But there's no sign of him."

"Look, it's not all that easy...."

When he was alone, absorbed in his thoughts, Hugo was able to control himself. But with Germain there it was too much. He paced back and forth, checking his address book, looking for a phone number. He was incapable of standing still, and the colossus moved away. He wanted to see the warehouse, he wanted to form a clear picture before the animal arrived.

It smelled new. Everything was clean and terribly sad. They would have to put in some windows, get their hands on some straw, pipe in water and erect a wall to mark off the animal's quarters and the rehearsal area. Germain was disappointed. He didn't like this place, and that upset Hugo even more. But he'd committed himself to do the job and he had just one thing to say.

"Did you order your big top by phone, like the elephant?"

Grumbling, he went back to the truck for his equipment: a pitchfork, buckets in various sizes, a hose, two bales of hay and some blankets.

In the midst of disaster, Hugo was calculating the extent of the work to be done. His peaceful days in the blue living-room or in front of the air conditioner now seemed so simple, so restful. He was about to sink into daydreams when the blast of a truck horn made him jump. Germain was there, at the back of the hangar. Hugo picked up his feet and raced outside.

Danby's trailer could be categorized as picaresque art.

On the sides of the big cube on wheels, the animal's life was recounted like that of a hero, an adventurer who had left Africa for countries unknown. The paintings were very garish on the red background, and Hugo barely noticed McTavish, the second-hand dealer. He came up to him, holding a docket.

"Mind giving me a little autograph?"

"Show me the animal first."

Germain came out too. McTavish had his back to him and hadn't seen him. He insisted that Hugo sign.

"No charge for the trailer," he said. "And I'll have you know, sir, that is art!"

Germain pounded on the side of the trailer and the second-hand dealer spun around, alarmed. The colossus was already at work opening the rear door.

"What's all this about a bump?" Hugo asked again.

"Nothing. Nothing at all," he stammered.

There was a foul smell as soon as Germain dropped the main panel. A dark grey mass was lying there in the shadows. Nothing was moving. It was hard to envisage the elephant depicted on the trailer.

"She's a little bit out of it," said McTavish. "Travelling wears them out."

"So it's a she," Hugo observed.

The second-hand man was clearly not as deaf as he had seemed. Sweat stood out on his forehead. Nothing was happening as he'd anticipated. That intimidating giant was in the trailer and he was sparing no effort.

"Hey! This animal's pregnant! She's about to give birth!"

McTavish pretended not to hear and again held out his docket to be signed.

"This is scandalous!" Germain bellowed. "That elephant has no business here! She needs care and attention!"

He was making such a racket in the trailer that Danby had started to move. Half standing on her forelegs, she heaved a sigh, as if somebody, finally, was going to do something about her.

"You sure about that? I didn't notice anything. You wanted an elephant and that's what I brought you."

Hugo's nervousness, the jitters he'd been experiencing lately, was transformed into a wave. A rumbling that rolled inside him and washed away everything that got in its way. His anger at Victor Daguerre, at forgetfulness, at contempt. His fury at this man who had lied to him. A tornado that swooped down on McTavish's shoulders.

Hugo was yelling so loudly that Germain came out to see what was going on. The second-hand dealer was packing up, heading for the truck. But the giant was blocking his way.

"Where do you think you're going? What do you intend to do with this animal?"

The man was confused. Hugo's hair was standing up on his head and he was howling like the damned. McTavish thought he was dealing with a lunatic. But Germain's size urged him to be extremely cautious.

"Now, you listen to me," said the giant.

The man they had thought to be deaf was suddenly all ears.

"You have to find her a place to give birth. And fast."

Without another word, Germain climbed into the truck and got into the passenger seat.

"I'm coming along. I want to be sure...."

McTavish didn't know which one scared him more, the big one or the little one. Hugo's nerves were frayed. He stood in front of the truck, spitting out insane remarks, while the giant was still worrying about the animal. McTavish got behind the wheel, because it struck him as the lesser evil, and started the engine.

When the truck with its wild trailer drove off down the street, Hugo heaved a long sigh. The circus had come very close, but now it was moving away.

Chapter 24
The Bookseller

He was wrapped in Marthe's arms as in a shroud. Turbaned, swaddled for all eternity and with no desire to be resurrected, to rise from the dead and get back into harness. Hugo had pulled the blanket over his shoulders. He had clung to her and now he was no longer stirring. After giving up the motel, he had given up the sofa. Ever since the expedition to the industrial park, he slept only with her.

He had come back from the hangar in bits and pieces. Not only had this deal cost him his last few dollars, but he had seen in Danby, the second-rate circus animal, a caricature of what he himself would become one day if he persisted in putting on this act.

The rest of the adventure had been epic. For one entire day Germain and the second-hand dealer had driven around in the truck looking for a spot to "place" the animal.

With its little anarchy, the house on Éliane Street satisfied Hugo completely. Ever since he'd discovered the swings in Marthe's apartment, ever since he'd learned to join her on the trapeze, the same thrill recurred every night. He would climb slowly up the stairs, he would pause for a moment in the doorway. The big top was inside, and so was Marthe.

Each time, he advanced onto the little platform, being very careful not to look down. The Lexiphone would be playing by itself, the music would be inviting, and all night long they would waltz. All night long they would fly beneath the roof of the big top.

*

In the morning, when Hugo opened his eyes, he looked for the trapeze, the spotlights and Marthe's blue leotard. All had disappeared, as they had on the previous days. Nothing remained of their lovemaking, of their tenderness ... nothing except the Lexiphone, maybe, stowed neatly in its case.

Marthe smiled in her sleep. She was happy, even blissful. Hugo looked around this bedroom that had once been Victor Daguerre's. One stage set always conceals another, and he got up on tiptoe.

Taking his pants off the dresser, he shook his head like a swimmer emerging from the water. Being in Marthe's arms was heaven, but when he stayed there too long he was seized with doubt. Life could not be this simple. Surely there was some trick, something she hadn't told him.

Downstairs in the living-room he was amazed at all the books lying around, which had accumulated this past while. And Marthe was still bringing down more. It was that time of year. In September the people in the neighbourhood went back to reading. As they always asked for the same titles again, she was just as glad to have them close at hand.

As trying as the expedition to the industrial park had been, Hugo was quick to clear it from his mind. He and Charlie had been reconciled as soon as he came back to the house. Marthe had brought out her white tablecloth and cooked up a delicious meal. To distract them, she had talked about an idea she'd been toying with for a while. To turn the main floor of the house into a reading-room. Build big shelves for the books, invite people to read them on the spot.

Hugo had grabbed hold of this idea like someone hurling himself at a lifebuoy. The failure of his own undertaking would seem less bitter if he had another project in the works. Not that he had the soul of a bookseller, mind you, but he enjoyed greeting people at the door, making them comfortable and finding the book they were looking for.

Leaning against the kitchen door, Hugo looked at the living-room from a distance. If he screwed up his eyes he could see a book-filled steamship sailing on calm water. Marthe had thought of everything. It would be a pleasant spot with armchairs here and there, a catalogue of the books and the register of loans and returns. No counter, nothing formal. As if people were in their own houses, reading books that belonged to someone else.

Marthe would offer individual service, suggesting titles, giving advice, but above all she would help people discover the treasures in Victor Daguerre's book collection. Like a guide, an outstretched hand.

He looked around the living-room and saw exactly

what Marthe was offering. A circus, in short — but a circus of words. The public would be there. All that was left to do was win them over, appeal to them, show them books as they'd never been shown books before.

Hugo was thrilled at the idea. So thrilled that he didn't hear the door creak in the front hall. He hoped Marthe would come down so they could talk about it some more. But it was Charlie who took him by surprise:

"Imagine the magic...."

It was only Thursday, but he had a suitcase in one hand and the Baudelaire in the other. In the little square, Jean-Philippe's car was driving away.

"My father said it's okay. I'll go back to his place next week, but that's the last time. Everything's settled."

"I see! So you're coming back for good?"

"... didn't Mama tell you?"

He set his suitcase by the stairs and sat down in the living-room, on the big sofa. The page of his book was turned over. He settled into the cushions and took up his reading where he'd left off.

"Is that you, Charlie?" asked Marthe from upstairs.

"Yes."

She raced down the stairs, threw herself on the sofa and kissed him exuberantly. The boy let himself be caught up in the game, dropped the silky-paged book onto the table and cuddled his mother too.

It was the first time Hugo had seen them snuggling together, rolling in the cushions. Discreetly he went back to the dining-room, where he examined the boy's suitcase. It was like a smaller version of his own: poorly closed, with clothes hanging out on either side, as if they'd been thrown in every which way. For a long time he had packed this way too. A ball, a tangle of rags. Then in the circus he had learned. Travelling had imposed a certain discipline.

In the kitchen, Hugo poured coffee beans into the grinder. The phone rang just as he turned it on. Cacophony. He set the grinder on a corner of the table but got tangled up in the cord. Half-ground coffee spilled onto the floor and finally it was Marthe who answered.

"Ah, Germain! We were just talking about you yesterday."

Charlie closed his book. He had enjoyed his mother's kisses, but news about the elephant was even better. He straightened up in the cushions and straddled the armrest while Hugo cleaned up his mess.

"I see, so she hasn't given birth yet?"

The colossus was talking very fast. Marthe kept covering the receiver to report what he was saying. An elephant's gestation period was twenty-odd months, they'd have to be patient. The vacationers would probably have time to leave. Danby would be able to give birth in peace.

Hugo went up to her. He wanted to have a word with the giant. Charlie climbed onto his mother, sticking his ear against hers, and it was chaos. Total anarchy around the sofa. But that was what was bringing them together. Together, they could laugh at anything.

*

The money from Barnum's arrived when Hugo was least expecting it. They had spent the weekend working on the layout for the living-room. Marthe had even drawn up a list of materials and made a rough budget. Then, on Monday, after taking Charlie back to his father's, they went into action.

But now here was Hugo burrowed into the sofa, turning the bank draft over and over in his hands. The money was there. A simple transfer would give him access to the funds, but he couldn't believe it. He looked all around him, seemingly numb.

The Lexiphone was still lying on the dining-room table, Marthe was putting the final touches to the plans and Hugo was laughing to himself, thinking about the fabulous acts he could have put on with this money. On the other hand, though, he had no regrets. It was great that Barnum's had paid him what he was owed. He'd made his choice.

Now he wasn't going to make an elephant dance in the ring; instead he would make books circulate through the neighbourhood. He and Marthe would restore life to the library that had been sleeping here for years. And they'd do it by the rule book.

Calculate the average thickness of a book multiplied by the approximate number of volumes in the collection. Around fifty shelves, a well-thought-out arrangement.

Marthe was a workaholic. When she put her mind to something, nothing else mattered. In fact, that was the way he liked her. And he got up to fetch the materials with her. But then heavy tears began to run down his cheeks. At first she thought he was playing the clown....

"Hey, what's going on?"

Hugo tried to laugh about it, to pretend. He waved the bank draft above his head, like the Statue of Liberty with her torch.

"Money! U.S.A! At last, free today!" he exclaimed in English.

But Marthe didn't believe a word. His eyes were wet, this was all an act. She came up to him very gently, took him by the shoulders and held him close. Only then did he acknowledge:

"It's you who affects me this way. You know perfectly well it's not the money!"

Chapter 25
The Blue Salon

There were construction materials all over the main floor. Dozens and dozens of shelving units had been delivered. They were all the same size; they just had to be assembled and fastened together, like a Meccano set.

Charlie was there, and he was there for good! Despite the pandemonium of building the reading-room, Marthe had found the time to meet with Jean-Philippe. Once again they had come to an agreement. The solution Charlie suggested was the best one. Why look for another?

There was no move as such. Hugo got out his suitcase and they travelled back and forth by taxi for three days. He liked making these round trips, and little by little they brought over all of Charlie's belongings.

Marthe was very careful not to interfere. It was a game. When they arrived at the house they would spread their booty on the dining-room table, put the suitcases back in the front hall for the next trip, then start racing all over the house. An hour later it was done. Everything had been put away!

In fact, over the few days the transaction lasted, Marthe made herself very discreet. While feigning interest in what they'd agreed to call the "Blue Salon," she didn't take her eyes off them. Later in the evening, alone in the bedroom with Hugo, she was still amazed.

"Do you realize? He's back. He's here! If it weren't for you, this would never have happened...."

"Don't exaggerate, Marthe. It's on account of you he came back."

"Before, he wasn't interested in anything. Now, though, if it's not the circus, it's Baudelaire. Have you heard the things he says sometimes, the words he comes out with just like that?"

"I'm behind in my own reading," said Hugo.

As they embraced, he complained that he no longer had access to Baudelaire. The book was practically forbidden to him. But she was laughing. At him, and at the two of them as well. At everything happening to them right now. On rainy evenings, they still leaned out the window together to howl into the lane. The month of August was bogged down in heat and humidity. The cool evenings of September were slow in arriving, but they had so much to do that they weren't even thinking about it.

The Blue Salon was in a way the solution to everything. Charlie, who had been lugging books for years, was still doing so, but now it was to fill the shelves. Marthe was amazing with a hammer. She took a fierce pleasure in putting up the shelves, as if it were something she'd been promising herself for ages. Nothing remained of the librarian with her hair in a bun whom Hugo had met one morning in June. Nothing of his half-sister, either, with whom he had shared Victor Daguerre such a long time ago.

Marthe had caught hold of all the little pieces of her

life, she was hammering them together, and to relax in the evening she made music. She played pieces that still had the same effect on Hugo. He would come upstairs, go into the bedroom and tenderly snuggle beside her.

They worked that way for a good week, not going out, not enquiring about what was going on in the outside world ... except maybe with Germain. Danby had regained her strength and her delivery was imminent. He and Gaël were awaiting the arrival of the baby elephant with curiosity. There would surely be a party to mark the blessed event, and they hoped that Charlie, Marthe and Hugo would attend. But there was so much to do, so many preparations before the Salon could open in early September....

Work began around eight in the morning. On the day in question, they were arranging the first bookcases in the Salon, so absorbed in their task that at first no one heard the knock at the door. It was Hugo who eventually stepped over the toolbox to go and open it.

He could already see the expression on the client's face. Madame Blanche, maybe. She wouldn't believe her eyes. Even if the work was still incomplete, she'd be flabbergasted. He opened the door, holding back a smile.

"Nothing is vorse than everything!" muttered the little man standing on the doorstep.

Marthe and Charlie, unaware of what was going on, continued hauling books and paid no attention to Hugo. He wished he could turn around, go back to them. But his knees were knocking. Feeling a burst of heat rise to his face, he grabbed hold of the doorknob to keep from falling.

The expression on Bobby's face was neither severe nor threatening. Actually, he too was white — and just as alarmed as Hugo. Not one word came out of his mouth.

Time stood still; the moment seemed endless. And then the knife-thrower stuck his hand inside his jacket and took out something shiny.

"No! Not that!"

Marthe turned her head abruptly. Charlie was already running towards the front hall, but too late! Hugo had collapsed in a heap! Facing him, Bobby still held the shiny object in his hand.

*

When Hugo opened his eyes, the first person he saw was Charlie. Convinced that they'd travelled together to the depths of the abyss, he closed them again. Bobby's knife had got the child too, the floor must be awash in blood.

Anger swept over him. It was one thing for the murderer to pursue him from one end of North America to the other, to stab him here on his doorstep, but harming the child was something else. It was intolerable!

"Hugo, you have to get up! You have to get to your feet!"

This had a strange effect on him. Charlie was calm and he was running his hand through his hair. He was very affectionate.

"Upsy-daisy! On your feet!"

A second voice joined that of the child.

"It's nothing. Just a brooch he wanted to give you. A piece of jewellery that belonged to...."

Hugo brought his hand to his heart, then to his belly. There were no wounds. And Charlie was becoming more and more insistent.

"Get up ... the man wants to talk to you!"

Bobby apologized effusively, but Hugo still couldn't move, so firmly did he believe he was dead, and Charlie couldn't take any more.

> "like an ecstatic swimmer in the sea
> you cleave, delighted, the transparent space...."

The boy was laughing. The transparent space was nothing but the front hall, the dagger just a piece of jewellery!

"I'm very, very sorry," said Bobby, stepping back onto the veranda. "I didn't mean to scare you like that!"

His dismay was absolutely real. The man was stammering, unable to say a word. The brooch was burning his fingers, and abruptly he turned towards Marthe to hand it to her. Hugo stood there motionless, and in a gesture of apparent good faith the other man bent down to him.

"Go ahead, my friend. You have to get up. Nothing is vorse than everything!"

Marthe was watching them in silence. This man was obviously the one Hugo had told her about. Yet he was quite unlike anything he'd said about him. Much smaller, not nearly as imposing. This Bobby was frail, and when Hugo finally got to his feet he started making bows.

"I am truly sorry, my friend. I didn't mean to scare you like that."

They were standing in the front hall. Marthe suggested they go inside. Charlie was hovering around them.

"Did you used to work in the circus with Hugo?"

"Leave him alone, Charlie, leave him alone!"

Bobby became vaguely interested in the boy. But he had his own peculiar way of speaking, a mixture of accent and shyness, and when he spoke only Hugo understood him.

"You must excuse us," announced Marthe, leading the way. "We're working on a project here just now."

They all gathered around the table; she made coffee, and it was Bobby who first made reference to the accident in Oakland. Marthe tried to get the child out of the way, suggesting he go and read in the living-room or his bedroom. Charlie totally ignored her.

"When I got to Chicago they told me you'd disappeared. I thought you were dead."

"That's more or less it, yes...."

"The accident was enough, don't you think?"

Hugo didn't bat an eye. This was the second time in as many sentences that the man had used the word "accident" and Hugo showed no reaction. For Marthe, who wasn't missing a word of the conversation, there was no end to astonishment. Not only did Bobby not resemble the portrait Hugo had painted, but the Oakland tragedy might not have occurred exactly as he'd said either.

In fact Hugo wasn't reacting to anything. He was relieved, glad it was over. Bobby was standing there in front of him. He had no intention of killing him. And oddly enough, he seemed more frightened than Hugo.

Marthe was doing all she could to make the moment pleasant. She served food and drink. The silences were sometimes very long, and then someone would say something.

"I looked for you, you know. I hung around in Florida for a month. I had the address of a bank, a branch in Tampa. But nobody there knew you!"

Hugo regained his composure. The fog of the first few moments had dissipated. He looked at Bobby and wondered why he'd been so afraid of this man.

"... but now it's better," he said. "It's fine. I've found you again and we'll be able to work."

"No, not me. I'm fine here where I am."

"What do you mean, not you? A thirty-year-old with a job with Barnum and Bailey doesn't retire!"

"Thirty-three. I'm thirty-three now," said Hugo.

"It's the same thing!"

Bobby had recovered too. He was very agitated, very worried about Hugo's attitude. As for Charlie, he was gasping with pleasure. He was hearing all of it and he was absolutely dazzled. Short of arguments, Bobby turned to Marthe.

"You know, he's one of the greats of the circus! A 'natural,' as the Americans say. He's funny. Very, very funny."

Marthe didn't doubt that. She was well aware of it herself. But it was the incident in Oakland that intrigued her. They had barely touched on the subject but one thing was certain, there was nothing of the killer about Bobby, and if he had followed Hugo here it wasn't because he was after his hide.

"He has to come back to the circus, madame. You have to make him understand that!"

Marthe's gaze went from one to the other. Bobby was sincere, you could see that, while a veil of mystery hung over Hugo's face.

"Why would I go back to the circus?" he asked. "Marthe and I are working on a project in the living-room."

With surprising courtesy, Bobby then bowed to her.

"You're called Marthe. It is a pretty name."

He had lovely manners, a little old-fashioned. He was a charming man and she held out her hand to him.

"Yes, my name is Marthe ... I'm a friend of Hugo's. An old friend."

He took her hand and kissed it. Flattered, she turned and beckoned to her son.

"And this is Charlie!"

"And my name," Bobby stated immediately, "is Lazlo Tisza. I'm Bulgarian, but around the Americans it was better to be a gypsy."

Hugo shuddered slightly. Lazlo who? He had never heard this name before, or anything about his being Bulgarian, either. Charlie, who had been holding his tongue for too long, took advantage of Hugo's surprise to ask:

"What do you do in the circus, sir?"

"I'm a knife-thrower!"

The question had seemed innocuous. They froze at the answer. Charlie was the first to regain the power of speech.

"A knife-thrower! Wow! I'd really like to try that!"

Chapter 26
"Invitation to the Voyage"

Hugo lied to me. He didn't tell me the whole truth. Since Lazlo Tisza, alias Bobby, has been with us, they talk about it often. Each of them assumes his share of the responsibility. First that code of conduct, that agreement never to raise their heads, never to look. Which was what Hugo had done that evening in Oakland. Apparently the knife-thrower had been distracted.

The strangest thing of all is that Hugo disputes none of this. In fact, Bobby sees to that himself. He willingly admits that he was jealous ... but who wouldn't have been jealous of Sally? He drank, too. He admits that. He'd sometimes drink before the show. But that evening he hadn't had a drop. He had flown into a rage, he'd yelled at his niece, but he hadn't had a drop. And even on that score, Hugo agrees.

They spend hours re-creating the incident, leaving nothing to chance. They turn the question over and over until they're dazed. But they come back to the same point every time. That night in Oakland, everything that wasn't supposed to happen did happen. If the one had contained his anger, if the other hadn't raised his head, if they both hadn't loved Sally so much. If, if, if....

Lazlo has taken over the sofa. The work in the Blue Salon has broken off, but they've both promised to help me tomorrow in finishing assembling the shelves and putting away the last of the books.

I'd imagined them incapable of getting along, sworn enemies, mired in rivalry. Yet they're always together, like the closet of friends. Sometimes for a change they'll talk about the circus, about the act Lazlo would like to put on. At first Hugo didn't want to hear a word about it. He'd made his choice. He would stay here, looking after the books. Now he's stopped putting up any resistance. He talks about it as if it were a game. He adores thinking up the ideal act.

Lazlo has been with us now for nearly three days. I've become fond of him. Charlie too, actually. He knows lots of stories, he tells all kinds of anecdotes about Hugo, about his talent and the crowds that used to collapse with laughter over his antics. He hasn't told me everything, of course, but then maybe I wasn't paying attention. The artist Lazlo talks about, the crowd-pleaser, has totally escaped me. It doesn't matter. At night when I play the Lexiphone, he leaves Lazlo downstairs and comes and joins me. I play that same piece, the one he likes, and he comes and prowls around me.

"My sister, my child
Imagine the magic
of living together
there, with all the time in the world
for loving each other,
for loving and dying...."

I play with my eyes shut. He doesn't touch me, but I know he's there. The bed makes waves, we can hear the water lapping:

> "On these still canals
> The freighters doze,
> their mood is for roving,
> and only to flatter
> a lover's fancy
> have they put in from the ends of the earth."

You might think the wolf is in with the sheep. Lazlo Tisza has set out to convince Hugo. He wants to take him back to the circus. I should be trying to keep him here, but I don't, not at all. I play the Lexiphone instead.... And he comes to me, he comes to sleep at my side.

> "By late afternoon
> the canals are ablaze
> as sunset glorifies the town;
> the world turns to gold
> as it falls asleep
> in a fervent light...."

I know that he'll leave, he'll go back to the circus. He made a name for himself in the States. He became somebody, apparently. That too he forgot to tell me. But Lazlo Tisza has taken that on. He'll go away, I love him, and I want to go with him. I'm waiting for him to invite me. Victor Daguerre's house can wait. So can the rest of the world. Charlie would like to come on the voyage too. He wants to put on an act. He's convinced there's a place in the circus for Baudelaire.